A PICTURE OF MURDER

DI GILES BOOK 15

ANNA-MARIE MORGAN

ALSO BY ANNA-MARIE MORGAN

In the DI Giles Series:

Book 1 - Death Master

Book 2 - You Will Die

Book 3 - Total Wipeout

Book 4 - Deep Cut

Book 5 - The Pusher

Book 6 - Gone

Book 7 - Bone Dancer

Book 8 - Blood Lost

Book 9 - Angel of Death

Book 10 - Death in the Air

Book 11 - Death in the Mist

Book 12 - Death under Hypnosis

Book 13 - Fatal Turn

Book 14 - The Edinburgh Murders

Book 15 - A Picture of Murder

Copyright © 2021 by Anna-marie Morgan

All rights reserved.

No part of this book may be reproduced in any form or by any electronic or mechanical means, including information storage and retrieval systems, without written permission from the author, except for the use of brief quotations in a book review.

For my son, Christopher

PROLOGUE

He stared down from the cliff edge at Constitution Hill, contemplating the threshing torrent of flesh-chilling water, whose wild motion tossed up frothing walls of foam that would engulf him, securing his end.

He had accepted it. There would be no more fighting. The gnawing futility had finally got to a young man of thirty-seven. Hot sweat, exuded in the struggle, felt like ice as the wind whipped him with his own clothing. The story of Guy Davies would take its place on the shelf amongst so many others who didn't make it.

Perhaps his family would keep his memory alive for a while, ensuring no-one forgot him, at least not this year.

He saw his best friend in primary school running away, challenging him to a race. And the mound of dirt in a corner of the playground, from where he would shout to anyone listening that he was the king of the castle. His first kiss at thirteen with the gangly, bespectacled Renita, who was a year older than him, stolen behind the school canteen. The exams, societies, college, and graduation, and a job in the council Town Planning Department. Was it enough the totality of this brief life lived?

His body shook, teeth clacking with thoughts of his mother and her quiet dignity as she turned a careworn face to the wind, salt-laden tears dropping into the surf as they dragged his body in. And they would haul it in. Eventually.

His killers hoisted him high. Guy closed grey-blue eyes, no longer straining the zip ties around his wrists or attempting to scream past the dirty rag they had stuffed in his mouth, held in place by round upon round of duct tape.

The condemned man held his breath until the last of his bones broke on the rocks below.

1

GRAVES OF THE VANISHED

Crows circled above the trees, chasing a war-scarred buzzard away from nests containing precious eggs.

Yvonne pushed her hands deep inside the pockets of her battleship-grey mac. Eyes fixed. Lips pursed. Face pensive.

Ahead of her, the grim task of recovering remains continued among the trees. Two mini-diggers and plastic-suited forensic officers delicately sifted soil, photographing each stage.

A man in overalls and wellingtons probed the surrounding area with an electrical resistance meter, using his boots to push the probes along its length into the ground as though he was using a garden fork. The instrument enabled them to visualise the topography below ground, and any further grave sites.

She shuddered. "I hope there are no more," she said aloud.

"I'm sorry?" Dewi flicked her a look, his usual suit jacket absent in favour of a wax coat that was the colour of the wet cowpats they had passed as they traversed the field en route to the site. Or, at least, that's what the DI had earlier told her sergeant, in teasing revenge for a comment he had made about her boots.

She nodded towards the makeshift graves. "I hope we don't find more bodies... I pray there are no more left to be found," she clarified.

Her DS pressed his lips into a thin line and sighed, nodding his head. "I know, two is more than enough."

The sky grew dark, as bulbous clouds held them all to ransom.

Yvonne pushed the collar up on her coat. "I also hope the rain holds off until they finish over there."

Dewi shrugged. "They have the marquee if they need it."

"We haven't." She cast him a sideways glance. "It's cold suddenly." Her eyes flicked back to the recovery operation and the two SOCO measuring the ground with a tape measure.

"You're right, it has, but there is always the car. We can shelter there, if we need to." He grinned at her. "You would have thought a sunny day was all wrong under the circumstances. I know you would."

She smiled, her expression softening. "You know me too well, Dewi Hughes."

"I do, ma'am."

∼

Eighteen-year-old Helen Carter took a large gulp of the cheap white wine purchased earlier that evening as she waited for her best friend, Victoria Mason. Once arrived, they could finish their last-minute prep for a weekend trip to AberFest music festival, on the Welsh coast.

Helen's dad Pete, a PE teacher at a local comprehensive,

would give them a lift in the family's people carrier. He preferred to check the venues his daughter frequented, himself. Safety first. And, although it grated with Helen's independent streak, she tolerated the intrusion for the ride. Neither she nor her friend had the money needed for a taxi, and they didn't fancy carrying the tent, clothes, and equipment onto public transport. And he was okay, really, and far cooler than Victoria's dad, Berwyn, an entrepreneur who believed in sharp suits and even sharper rules. No, her dad was one of the good guys, and she secretly liked the fact he was looking out for her.

She checked her outfit in the mirror. They were expecting high temperatures over the weekend. Pundits predicted them to break all records for the middle of June. So sleeveless would be the order of the day. Vest tops and cut-off shorts, long necklaces and bangles.

They were expecting to share a few drinks with others, once her dad had helped them erect the tent, and the evening would be warm and long.

When Victoria arrived fifteen minutes later, Peter Carter had already packed the car, and Helen was hugging her mum, Celia, goodbye.

Both girls rushed around, their excitement palpable. It was going to be a glorious weekend.

Carter threw the last of the bags into the boot, stretching to relieve the stiffness in his wide shoulders. At forty and six-foot-two, he could handle most things, and still worked out at the local gym, playing golf with Vicky's father, Berwyn, two weekends in every month. All this, on top of the school's energetic PE schedule. But it was a far-cry from the county rugby he had played as a lad. A compound fracture of his right thigh had wrecked his dreams of playing for the national team. Intensive physiotherapy had helped him heal well-enough, but the psychological aftermath of the injury had left him with a fear of getting stuck in. So, he had given up rugby and taken up general fitness instead. The girl's luggage caused him little trouble.

He leaned against the vehicle, waiting for the two excited teenagers to finish getting ready. He knew better than to rush either of them. Anyway, if he was honest, he was happy hanging onto his only girl for a little while longer, putting off the anxiety. Not that he worried as much as his wife, Celia. Celia Carter could worry for Wales. No, he liked to think that his fatherly concern was in perspective, and necessary for a daughter in the modern world.

As the three of them set off for the coast, the girls laughing in the back, Pete Carter smiled to himself. He was proud of his family and the life he had built.

2

DEATH ON THE ROCKS

Spray filled her nostrils, and the tang of fish clung to hair that whipped around her face in the fierce sea breeze.

Yvonne pursed her lips, squinting from the glare of the sun off the sea.

They had found three sets of remains in as many weeks. Investigators suspected that the body being hauled in now was that of thirty-eight-year-old Guy Davies from Newtown, who had been missing for four days. The dead man's clothing — long black coat, green t-shirt, and jeans — matched those witnesses had described seeing Guy wearing on the day he disappeared.

Dewi joined her on the rocky beach at the foot of Constitution Hill. "It looks like murder." He flicked his head toward search and rescue, as they stretchered the body towards a waiting ambulance. "Whoever killed him tied his hands behind his back."

She grimaced. "Do they think someone dumped him on the rocks?"

Her sergeant shook his head. "The body has extensive

injuries. A lot of broken bones." He glanced up at the cliff. "I think they pushed him off the top."

"Oh, God..." She pursed her lips. "Poor bugger..."

"We should have the postmortem results later tomorrow."

"I hope he didn't suffer."

Dewi nodded. "A fall from that height onto boulders? It would have been quick. I doubt he knew much about it after he landed. Beforehand, however..." There was little need for him to say more. Both were aware the victim had spent several days with his abductors. Anything could have happened prior to his death at the foot of the cliff and, whereas others could protect themselves from the full knowledge of what had taken place, it was their job to face those horrors head-on, exposing the truth. Whatever that might be.

The crime scene was problematic, as the sea had likely destroyed crucial forensic material. The DI hoped the victim hadn't been in the sea for long, providing the best chance of saving some of that critical evidence.

As two rescuers stretchered Guy's body to the waiting ambulance, picking their way through the rocky terrain, Yvonne and Dewi made their way past the CSI van and the rest of the SOCO team, leaving them to their work. The detectives' job was to learn as much as they could about Guy Davies' life, and what might have led to his becoming a murder victim.

As they headed inland, they spotted two women watching them from the end of the promenade, over the battered railings that ran the length of the low wall below Constitution Hill.

One woman had her arm around the shoulders of the

other, whose tear-stained face gazed at them, wide-eyed and expectant.

Uniformed officers had explained that Guy's mother and aunt were in attendance and waiting for information. The DI guessed they were the two waiting by the wall. News had travelled fast.

She took a deep breath and approached them. "Martha Davies?" she asked, resisting the urge to extend her hand. COVID-19 was still a pervasive threat, and the country was only now emerging from the latest lockdown as they approached Easter.

The tearful woman nodded, letting out a sob. "I'm praying it isn't my son."

The DI pressed her lips together, her eyes lowering to the sand-strewn tarmac, before returning to the stricken mother's face. "I know, I hope that too... for your sake." She sighed. "We will require you for a formal identification." She rubbed the back of her neck. "If it is your son, we'll be asking you about his life. And, I can promise you, we will do everything in our power to find out what happened to him. If someone else caused his death, we will bring them to justice."

Martha ran a handkerchief over her eyes, holding her wayward grey hair with the other hand. She shivered, despite the yellow raincoat she wore zipped to her chin, and the tartan scarf around her neck. Martha's equally grey-haired sister held the crying woman as though to protect her from the devastating news that seemed inevitable. That, and the wind whipping in from the sea.

As Yvonne and Dewi made their way along the prom to their car, The DI's heart weighed heavy in her chest. The chance that the victim was not Martha's son was slim, but she understood the mother's need to cling to the tiny sliver of hope left.

∼

The mortuary lights beamed down on Guy Davies' body as Roger Hanson's assistant readied the instruments for his postmortem.

Yvonne checked her watch. Hanson was late, probably held up in traffic following the accident she had heard about on the Newtown bypass.

The victim's skin was a myriad colours from the contused lacerations incurred during the fall.

The DI swallowed a lump in her throat as she hung up her coat on one of the chrome pegs near the door.

Hanson rushed in, panting as he gave her a nod. "Yvonne," he said, discarding his coat and case before disappearing into a side room to scrub up.

She knew this was his way of apologising for keeping her waiting. He wasn't a man to waste time on needless words. When he spoke again, it would be as he examined and excised organs from the body lying on the cold metal trolley.

That suited Yvonne, who was not in the mood for small talk. She had heard of postmortems full of banter, laughter, and even the eating of sandwiches, something she could not countenance herself, believing firmly in the utmost respect for the dead. She was glad that Roger Hanson was from the same mould. His was a banter-less mortuary.

Hanson cleared his throat. "As you know, they bound the victim's hands behind his back with zip-ties. There was a rag in his mouth, held in place by a ring of duct tape, which they wound several times around the victim's head and mouth. Forensics have the bindings. The victim also sustained multiple bruises, cuts, and torn clothing."

Hanson continued, "The first thing to note is the massive skull fracture." He grunted. "Severe, blunt head trauma was likely to have been the fatal injury. It's the most common cause of death in cliff falls." He peered at her over his glasses, scratching his cheek with his shoulder. "I must warn you, Yvonne, this won't be pretty."

She took a deep breath. "I know."

He spoke aloud as he worked, noting a fractured sternum, cardiac rupture, a lung injury, a fractured left hip and femur, fractures to both humeri, fractured clavicles, severe intracranial bleeding, and a subdural haematoma on the side of the brain opposite the skull damage.

"Could any of these injuries have occurred prior to the fall from the cliff?" she asked.

Hanson pursed his lips. "Hard to say for sure if there was bruising or even fractures immediately prior to the fall. However, I can say that all the fractures appear fresh. There was no time to heal. The body spent a while in the sea, and much of the blood had washed away. The absence of water in the lungs suggests he was dead before the tide came in. Decomposition has set in, making it difficult to determine when he sustained the bruising. What I see, however, is consistent with a fall from a height onto large rocks. A closer examination of the bones themselves, may tell us more. But this was murder... right? I mean, hands tied behind his back isn't something that a suicide would do. Gagged with duct tape? It's a deliberate act."

She nodded. "I wanted to know if they tortured him first, before throwing off the cliff."

"Of course. Do you have any suspects? We should have his nail swab results back soon. Maybe he scratched his kidnappers. And the duct tape, we may have fibres and DNA. It's an unusual crime."

She shook her head. "We don't have anyone in the frame, yet. We'll need all the clues that you and SOCO can glean, but I'll wager its someone he knew. Maybe he got himself caught up in something he couldn't get out of. We know that gang crime has been increasing in the area. We'll question those who knew him tomorrow. His mother is distraught."

Hanson nodded, peeling off his gloves. "Thirty-eight is no age at all."

"It isn't."

~

As she walked to her car, Yvonne pondered Guy's last moments, wondering if he had got himself mixed up in the County Lines drugs scene.

Opening her vehicle door, she shrugged. Time would tell, and she would ensure that it coughed up everything.

3

ABERFEST

The sun shone hot in a cobalt sky. All across the field shirts were coming off, tossed to the ground amongst leftover beer cans and food packets.

Around them, the crowd writhed and jumped to the sounds emanating from the stage, its semi-circular hulk like a giant open clam. Hearts throbbed in time with the music.

Helen grinned at her best friend Victoria as she waved her hands high in the air and bounced up and down in a neon-green tank top. "Woo!" She threw her head back. Long dark hair stuck to her face. "I love this one," she called, referring to the song that was starting up.

Victoria joined in with her, jumping with the beat and losing the straw hat from her head. Wavy, ash-blonde hair thrashed around her face. She stopped to tie the bottom of her t-shirt, allowing air to cool her midriff. "I need a drink."

When the song ended, the girls reached for beers from their cool box, pouring the liquid into mandatory plastic containers, trying to spill as little of it as possible. Vicky opened up a red backpack to check her phone. No messages. Shrugging her shoulders, she zipped it back up.

As they each guzzled half of their respective drinks, carried away by the music and the moment, they failed to see the would-be predator approaching from behind. They placed the drinks on the ground next to the backpack and carried on dancing.

Glancing around, he dropped a pill into each of the girls' tumblers, licking sweat from his upper lip as he waited for the fizzing yellow liquid to quiet.

The girls later drank it, oblivious. The beat and alcohol amplified their giddy sense of happiness and freedom in what was their last summer before beginning courses at university in only a few short weeks.

They had chosen Liverpool. Helen, to study Botany; Victoria, Art and Design.

Those around watched the girls become increasingly intoxicated, their movements erratic as they gyrated over an ever-larger area.

Other revellers gave them a wide berth, staring at the spectacle the girls were making of themselves.

When Victoria keeled over into the dirt, those closest suspected she was drunk, not realising that it was only her second can.

A look of confusion clouded Helen's features as she helped her friend up. Moments passed until she, too, felt odd. Her head swam.

They stumbled toward the portable toilets at the edge of the field, lumbering through the crowd, pushing their hands out to steady themselves and avoid crashing into people.

As they approached the cubicles, Helen threw up on herself.

Both girls collapsed before reaching their destination.

4

GRIM DETAILS

Yvonne spread the photographs across her desk.

Two makeshift graves within a few feet of each other. The likelihood of it being different perpetrators was slim and, to her mind, impossible.

Someone had murdered two young women and buried them in Warren Wood.

The Pathologist confirmed the remains were of females in their late teens and had been in the ground for upwards of fifteen-to-twenty years. They were now mere skeletons, with only hair and heavily stained, torn clothing remaining. Their garments suggested someone had murdered them at the height of summer, though Crime Scene Investigation had not confirmed that.

The DI had the results of the DNA analyses, but was awaiting dental records. DCs Dai Clayton and Callum Jones trawled the MisPer register in the local area for the relevant timeframe.

"I bet he thinks he got away with it." Dewi joined her, handing over a hot mug of tea. "Twenty years, he'll have thought he was home and dry."

She nodded. "They found nothing else. There were no other graves up there, only those of the two girls."

"Perhaps, the killer specifically targeted them. Maybe, a domestic murder?"

"They're not siblings, not according to the DNA analysis."

"Friends, maybe?" Dewi took a mouthful of tea.

"Perhaps, they were enjoying a hot summer and met the wrong person. A sexually motivated crime is a possibility. They may have been at a beach party, or another gathering of some sort. We should get a better idea when we have their identities. How are you getting on with that?" She raised an eyebrow at him, as she discarded her black cardigan on the back of the chair.

"We may have the results from dental records by the end of the day." He frowned. "You know Hanson could only determine a cause of death for one of the girls. The murderer strangled her. He has requested the help of an anthropologist to analyse the bones of the other."

The DI nodded. "Well, at least we are a little further forward." Her eyes took on a faraway look as she pondered the women's last moments. "I wonder whether either of them knew what was coming?"

Dewi pursed his lips, saying nothing.

She understood. The thought that one of them might have witnessed the demise of the other was almost too grim to bear.

~

"Have we confirmed the identity of the male found at the bottom of the cliff?" DCI Chris Llewelyn strode up to her in the corridor outside of the incident room.

"We know who he is, sir. Or rather, who he was. We've confirmed him as Guy Davies. His aunt identified him on behalf of his mother, who passed out on the way into the chapel of rest."

"Oh..." He pressed his lips together. "Poor woman."

"It's every mother's worst nightmare." Yvonne ran a hand through her mussed blonde hair.

"And, how are you?" Llewelyn narrowed his eyes, scanning her face. "Is everything all right? Work? Home?"

"Of course, why?" She mirrored his half-closed lids.

"Just checking that my ace detective is fit and well." He grinned. "I'll leave you to get on."

Yvonne watched him walk down the corridor, hands in his trouser pockets, shirt sleeves rolled up to the elbows, humming to himself, looking for all the world like he had it easy. He didn't, but he was convincing, and instilled confidence. She admired him for that.

DC Callum Jones caught up with her as she approached the stairs down to reception. "Yvonne?"

She swung round, jolted from deep thought. "Yes?"

"We have the identities of the bodies from Warren Wood."

"You have? Great." She tapped him on the shoulder. "Well done, who were they?"

"Helen Carter and Victoria Mason, both eighteen, who disappeared in June of two-thousand. We have files on the disappearances from missing persons. There's a fair bit of info in them, but its limited because they didn't know for certain that foul-play was involved. Dewi might remember their cases." He grimaced. "It was before my time, I'm afraid."

"Where are the files now, Callum?"

"On your desk."

She checked the time. "I was on my way out, but I'll come back and have a look. I don't want to wait."

Callum accompanied her to the incident room.

They had a lot of material to sift through. It would take them most of the day to read witness statements, family information, and other details from what had been a thorough search for the girls at the turn of the millennium.

Amongst the myriad papers was a seven-by-eight inch photograph. It fell out of the sheaf Yvonne was holding as though calling for her attention.

She picked it up, turning it over to examine the words on the back, scrawled in pencil, 'Last known photograph of Helen Carter and Victoria Mason, 17th June 2000' and a name, 'Andrew Wyatt'.

She turned it around to scrutinise the image.

Someone had taken it at a festival. There were youngsters in a field, dressed in shorts, short skirts, skimpy tops, no tops, and having a great time, arms in the air and dancing.

Helen and Victoria were in the centre of the picture, eyes half-closed, lost in the music. They appeared to pay no heed to those around them who had moved back, providing a bigger circle to dance in. Several onlookers stood mesmerised, enjoying the spectacle. The DI counted five males watching. Six, if you included the photographer who could be the Andrew Wyatt named on the back.

Were any of those males involved in what happened to the girls? Had they liked what they saw and pushed it further?

She pursed her lips. The file would require a thorough read-through. She wanted the names and details of those men, and to interview all of them as soon as possible.

5

THE PHOTOGRAPH

The story of the lost girls of Warren Wood enthralled local and national news media. Their curiosity and thirst for information weighed heavily on the team. People wanted to know how the girls came to be buried in the wood. Why investigators had taken two decades to find them. They demanded the identity of the killer, and they all needed the inside story, now.

Yvonne waded through reporters and photographers to get into work the following morning. It was clear they were more interested in the cold case than they were in the recent crime of a young man being launched off a cliff with his hands trussed behind his back.

The DI and her murder investigation team were now tackling two separate enquiries, the events of which had occurred twenty-one years apart. It would stretch her officers to the limit. Reporters filling the carpark was the last thing they needed.

As soon as she had thrown her jacket over the back of her chair, she opened up the old missing person files for Helen and Victoria.

The pair had been friends since pre-school and were heading for the same university later that year. They had chosen Liverpool.

The DI noted the families' names and addresses, as she would need to interview them again, whilst respecting their need to grieve now that investigators had confirmed their daughters were dead.

Dewi joined her, pulling out statements from youngsters at the festival. Frowning in concentration, he perused them, tutting one moment and sighing at others. "According to this witness, they were playing to the crowd." He eyed Yvonne over his spectacles.

"What do you mean?" She leaned back in her chair, her thoughts about the parents' statements on hold.

"Their dancing was getting a little on the wild side before they headed off to the toilets." He tapped the paperwork. "One of them fell over and appeared very drunk."

Yvonne nodded. "That wouldn't surprise me. It was a festival, and it was hot. Everybody was drinking. I think many of those present would have ended up intoxicated. The girls were having a good time and were probably very excited about going to college and building lives of their own. Getting away from mum and dad. It would have been a heady mix."

"What about the parents? What did they have to say about the day they disappeared?"

Yvonne tilted her head, scratching her cheek. "Only what you would expect. They said there was nothing unusual about either of them. Helen's father drove them to the festival and left them there for the weekend. He was due to pick them up again the day after this photograph was taken." She handed the picture to Dewi. "The MisPer team only ever identified two of the males in that picture. Two out of five who were watching the women. I think we should speak to both, and to Andrew Wyatt, who snapped the image. Can you set up interviews with the girls' parents for us?" She rubbed her chin. "I'll get Callum and Dai onto finding these men, the known and the unknown."

"Right you are, ma'am." He nodded. "I'll continue wading through this lot for contact details."

~

IT TOOK two days to locate Andrew Wyatt.

Having lived in several places in the UK, he had returned to Wales and settled in Machynlleth, Powys, around an hour's drive south-west of Newtown.

Yvonne agreed to interview him at the outward bound centre he co-owned with his wife, Yvette.

Yvette Wyatt was not present at the glass-fronted centre, nestled amongst rolling hills and crags, which sported a cafe and restaurant to the front, a tiny bookshop to the rear, an equipment store, and lecture theatre. The setting was picturesque or barren, depending on your point of view. A peaceful place to live and work.

Andrew came out of the sliding doors to greet her as she parked the car.

She wondered if he had been watching for her. Business would be slack in the COVID-stricken era they inhabited. They had limited movement around Wales to a five-mile radius in urban areas, with only a little leeway given in more rural parts, such as the one in which Machynlleth, a small market town built of dark Welsh stone, lay.

'Outward Bound' was a mile and a half further on from the town, in a westerly direction, towards the coast.

He offered to take her shoulder bag.

She declined.

"We're really quiet, as you can imagine." He tilted his head, closing one eye against the glare of the spring sunshine. "They keep giving us false hope," he added, referring to the governments's promise to businesses that things would soon open up again.

Wyatt looked younger than his forty-one years. Barely a grey hair and skin that was still smooth. Yvonne now sported several fine slivers of silver hidden amongst the blonde which her partner Tasha had told her was an endearing feature, even though the psychologist had barely a grey hair in her chocolate mop.

The outdoor life had benefitted Andrew Wyatt.

"Can I get you a coffee?" He asked as they entered the kitchen area.

Beyond the counter, she could see the few visitors who had ventured to the centre. They had probably come from the town and, likely, were only there for a change of scenery. They tucked into tea and sandwiches, all socially distanced at the requisite two metres, their masks lying on the table beside their plates.

"Thank you." She sat on a stool by the counter that he pulled out for her. "It must be difficult to stay afloat at the moment?"

He placed a small metal jug of milk under the hot jet of the coffee machine, waiting until the swooshing abated before replying. "We were lucky... Twenty-nineteen was an excellent year for us. We'd built up savings. But, yes, without government help and the furlough scheme for our staff, we could easily have gone under."

She nodded, taking out her notes. "Mister Wyatt, can I talk to you about Helen Carter and Victoria Mason?"

He paused, his back to her. She wished she could see his

expression. Her question should not have surprised him, Dewi had told Wyatt the reasons for the interview.

He continued pouring hot, frothy milk into the coffees, before loading the mugs and a plate of biscuits onto a tray. "Yes..." He didn't look at her. "I heard on the news that you had found them." He shook his head. "They seemed lovely girls. What a waste..."

"How long had you known them?"

"I didn't know them, not really. I met them, literally, at the AberFest music festival."

"You took this photograph." She opened her bag, taking out the image.

He accepted it from her, screwing his mouth up as he examined it. "I did... I remember it like it was yesterday. Tragedy does that to you, doesn't it? Makes you remember things in fine detail. They were all over the news a few days after I took this picture. Missing. Their parents were going out of their minds. I remembered the girls and got my film developed straight away so I could give that photo to the police officers who were looking for them."

"I see... Tell me about the day you took the photograph. Take me back to when you woke in your tent that morning."

He pressed his lips together, his eyes glazed over as he began recalling the details. "I woke early, just after five. The sun was up, and my tent felt like an oven. I set up my camping stove outside and got some coffee brewing and sausages cooking. The sky was clear, and it was pretty obvious the day was going to be a scorcher."

"And this was the Saturday morning?" The DI paused from her note-taking.

"Yes, Saturday, the seventeenth. I think the parents reported the girls missing on Sunday the eighteenth of June, but my interaction with them had been the day before, which was the Saturday."

"I see... Go on."

"I had one of the early digital cameras back then. Great big chunky thing, it was. I carried it around everywhere, preferring it to my lighter film camera because of the immediacy of the results. I could see straight away if I'd got an excellent shot, it was such a luxury."

"Did you intend publishing the pictures?"

Wyatt shook his head. "No, I was purely an amateur." He grinned. "I simply enjoyed taking photographs, though I did fancy taking up journalism one day. "

"When did you first meet Helen and Victoria?"

"It was early in the afternoon on the Saturday. I had been photographing the bands as they performed, snapping occasional pictures of the crowd when something interesting kicked off. I saw a circle opening up amongst a group who were dancing quite close to where I was, and I moved nearer to get a better look. I thought there might be a photo opportunity, and I was right."

"So, you noticed something unusual going on?"

"I did..."

"What did you see?"

"I saw two girls dancing in the centre of a circle, engrossed in the music. They were throwing themselves about a bit. I assumed, at that point, they were drunk. You know, eyes glazed, and they were stumbling about."

"What time would that have been?"

"I would put it around two in the afternoon... Perhaps a little later."

"Did you see them drinking alcohol?"

He turned his gaze skyward. "You know, I don't think I

did, but they had drinks near to them, so I think they had been beforehand."

"Can you remember what the drinks were?"

"Erm... Lager, I think. It certainly looked like lager to me. They were drinking from plastic pint glasses, and the liquid was yellow."

"So, you wouldn't be able to tell me how much they had consumed in total?"

He shook his head. "Officers asked me that, but I wasn't with the girls. I mean, I hadn't spent time with them, I was simply standing near to where they were. I can only tell you what I saw."

"Of course..." She tapped her pen against her lip. "You took the last known photograph of them before they vanished."

"I know." He sighed. "I thought about that a lot after they disappeared, and again last week, when you found their remains in the wood. As soon as I realised I had something that might be useful to the inquiry, I handed it in at my local police station."

"Sure." She nodded. "There are several people staring at the girls, in the photograph. Do you recall them?"

"Vaguely." He shrugged. "I can't say I was paying them much attention. My focus, just like theirs, was on the girls."

"Did you know any of the onlookers?"

He shook his head. "I'd never met them before. I explained that to the original investigators, who I think tracked down two of the guys. They ran an appeal and had a few people self-identify. I don't recall the names, I'm sorry."

"That's okay, we have the information from that inquiry, and the names and statements of those who helped." Her gaze wandered to the window and the hills outside. "I'm surprised that more didn't come forward. We'll be looking into those that didn't."

"Are you looking into me?" He asked, clearing his throat.

Her eyes swung back to his. "Should I be?"

"No, I just wondered if this interview was the end of it?"

She shrugged. "That will depend on what we uncover."

"I see." His eyes dropped to his hands.

"When was the last time you saw the girls? What happened when they stopped dancing?"

"They were bobbing around for about twenty minutes, before the fair-haired one fell. I think that's when they left to go to the toilets that were at the edge of the field, near the wood. Both of them were stumbling a bit, actually. I realised they had drunk more than I thought. There were a couple of beer tents and people had also taken along their own drinks in cool boxes and whatnot. So lots of people were getting merry, the girls were just having a good time like everyone else."

"Where were they when you last saw them?"

"They were heading through the crowd towards the Portaloos at the top of the field. They had their backs to me, and the dark one was helping the blonde one along."

"The dark one being Helen Carter?"

"I believe so, yes. Though I didn't know their names until afterwards."

"Were drugs being taken at the festival?"

"Probably, somewhere, but I didn't see anyone using. Well, I saw the odd joint, maybe. But, other than that, I didn't see drug use, and I saw nothing harder than cannabis."

"What about Helen and Victoria, did they smoke cannabis?"

He shook his head. "Are you asking if they were stoned?

I don't think so, I only saw them with drinks, they weren't smoking. I did see them take a swig of their lager, but that's all, and I watched them dance for around twenty minutes. They were really into the music."

"And you didn't see them again after they left for the toilets?"

"No, they vanished into the crowd, and that was that. I didn't see or hear anything of them again until their disappearance was reported on the news after I got home. I recognised the women right away. As I say, I got my photos printed as fast as I could, and got them down to the police station."

"It was a quick-thinking and helpful thing to do."

"Yes, but it didn't make any difference in the end, did it?"

Yvonne pursed her lips. "You never know, that photograph may yet help identify the girls' killer."

"I'd like that." He took a gulp of coffee. "They deserve justice."

"Did you have a girlfriend back then?"

"Me?" He frowned. "What do you mean? How is that relevant?"

The DI studied his face. "I was wondering, if you did, whether she might have something to add, any observations regarding the girls and their demeanour."

"Oh... Well, I didn't have a girlfriend, so you only have my perspective, I'm afraid."

She gave him a thin smile. "You've been very helpful, Mister Wyatt. Thank you, for your time."

He stood, extending his hand. "You're welcome."

"I'm sorry, COVID," she reminded him, declining the handshake.

"Of course." He pulled her chair back for the DI to get up, then saw her out.

6

A BITTER PILL

Yvonne took Dewi with her to speak to Pete Carter.
Dewi was the only member of her team who could remember the case of the vanishing girls first-hand, having been a young DC at the time they disappeared.

It had been the talk of the Dyfed-Powys force and, for a time, of the nation.

Although an appeal on the landmark TV programme Crimewatch had thrown up several avenues, each eventually ended in disappointment. The lead investigator at the time had been DC John Langford, now retired. Yvonne planned to speak with him soon, if he was willing. Cold cases were hard at the best of times. A few pointers from the original investigator would give them a head start. Some of a detective's suspicions never made it to a file. She had learned that early on. There were various reasons, but that didn't mean that those hunches weren't valid, just that there was not enough evidence to back up the gut instinct.

The Carters had moved home twice since their daughter Helen disappeared.

Back on the Welsh coast, their three-bed semi overlooked the harbour at Aberystwyth, the place from which their girl and her best friend vanished.

The DI guessed the need to feel connected with Helen drove this choice, and it was the place most likely to yield answers about her disappearance that fateful day in June.

Harbour View cottage stood at the bottom of a narrow lane running parallel to the coast road. In the shadow of the more imposing Georgian sea-front properties, the little beige-painted dwelling was a demure second-cousin, a tagger-on, but beautiful. The Carters ran it as a bed-and-breakfast, and the DI felt they had chosen a pleasant spot as it was quieter than the seafront, but close enough that visitors could be at the beach or a local restaurant within minutes.

Pete carter answered the door, looking relaxed in an open-necked, blue-check shirt and jeans, sleeves rolled up to his elbows. His dark hair, streaked with grey, had thinned on top.

Although the DI and her sergeant wore face masks, as per the COVID regulations, their host didn't. He showed them through to the conservatory at the back of the house where his wife Celia sat at a table near to a window over the harbour.

Several tables filled the room, none of which were dressed for guests.

Celia Carter stood as they entered. Unlike her husband, she wore a face mask, appearing tiny next to her broad spouse. She wore her ash-blonde hair in a bob.

Carter adjusted the seat cushions for his wife, as Yvonne and Dewi pulled back the two remaining chairs at the table for themselves.

"Thank you for agreeing to talk to us." The DI tilted her

head, her eyes flicking between the couple. "First, let me say how sorry we are about the devastating news. I know nothing I can say will make your loss any easier, but I wanted you to know that we will investigate your daughter's death with all the vigour we would bring to a fresh murder inquiry."

Pete nodded, his eyes drawn. The dark lines underlined their vivid green. "Some b..." He bit his lip. "Someone killed our daughter and her friend. We just want them dealt with."

Yvonne nodded. "We understand, and will do everything in our power to get justice for Helen and Victoria."

Celia Carter switched her gaze from the harbour to the DI at the mention of her daughter's name. When the Yvonne's eyes met Mrs Carter's, Celia returned hers to the boats moored in the harbour.

"Helen was our second child, you know?" Pete leaned his elbows on the table, his hands together as though in prayer.

Yvonne frowned. "Oh, I'm sorry," She looked at her notes. "I thought you only had-"

"One child?" he finished for her. "Our son, Michael, was stillborn." He pressed his lips together.

"Oh..." She closed her eyes for a moment. "I'm sorry..." To lose one child was bad enough, but two? She could only imagine their pain.

Pete Carter continued. "We were over the moon when Helen was born. We moved to Wales after we lost our son."

"Where were you before?"

"We have lived in a few places in England and Wales. Celia and I met while I was working as a young teacher in Burnley."

"I was working in the same school as an administrator," Celia explained.

Yvonne thought she recognised a lilt to Celia's voice. Though she appeared to have lost much of the accent. "And you fell in love." She smiled. "So, after your first loss, you moved to Wales?"

"Yes." Pete nodded, scratching the back of his head. "We came close to..." He looked at his wife.

Their eyes met, and she nodded, giving a two-lidded wink.

"We came close to splitting up out of grief." Carter sighed. "It was a really awful time. A fresh start helped us get through it and stay together, but then..." He bowed his head. "It was in Wales that we lost our daughter." He wiped his cheek with the back of his hand. "We lived in Dolgellau when it happened. Vicky's dad, Berwyn, still does. It's where our two girls grew up."

His wife's haunted face turned from the window to the detectives and her husband. "You can't escape fate, can you? No matter what you do..." Once again, her gaze returned to the harbour.

The DI pursed her lips, concerned for Celia's mental well-being. "Did our support officers get in touch?"

Carter sighed. "Victim liaison left their details and are coming here again tomorrow."

She nodded. "Good. Mister Carter, can you tell us how your daughter was prior to going to the festival? What was her mood? Was she happy? Concerned? Frightened?"

He tilted his head while he recalled. "She was happy. Both Helen and Vicky were excited about the festival, and college. They behaved just as you would expect two youngsters who had their entire lives ahead of them to..." His voice trailed away.

"I understand they were heading for Liverpool University later that year?"

"That's right, they were making the most of the time they had before their courses started."

"I'm sorry to ask, Mister Carter-"

"Pete."

"Pete... Would you have known if your daughter had gotten mixed up with the wrong crowd? Or, perhaps, dabbled in substance misuse?"

"What?" His forehead furrowed. "What do you mean? Helen wasn't that sort of girl."

She held up a hand. "I know, I am just exploring possibilities. We have information to suggest the girls were becoming unusually intoxicated. We are investigating whether someone administered the girls something without their knowledge."

"You mean like a date rape drug?"

"Yes, that sort of thing."

Carter gritted his teeth, his fists clenched on the table.

Celia Carter kept her gaze on the window.

The DI's voice was soft. "We really want to find your daughter's killer. I wouldn't ask anything I didn't think relevant."

He sighed. "I'm sorry."

"It's okay, you're Helen's dad. You want to protect her, and that includes safeguarding her memory. We get it, truly we do."

"I am very sure she wasn't into drugs. She wouldn't have taken any by choice."

"That's helpful, thank you."

He frowned again. "Wait, can't you test for substances, I mean toxicology stuff? Don't you do that on... on..." He couldn't bring himself to say the word bones.

She nodded. "We do, but your daughter's remains have been in the ground for a considerable time and, even if they hadn't, some substances used for subduing a victim can leave the system in a very short time, less than twenty-four hours with GHB. However, I can assure you we are conducting tests on the remains. If there are any such compounds present, we will find them, and inform you."

"I think the person who killed them was at that festival." Carter scowled. "I hate the thought that the killer watched them dancing, probably planning how he would attack and kill them as soon as he got the opportunity."

Yvonne sighed. "Yes, but you must focus on the positive memories of your daughter, and believe that we will do everything in our power to bring your daughter's killer to justice." She glanced over at the photograph of the smiling little girl on the windowsill. "You must have lovely memories. Hold on to those. Remember your beautiful daughter as she was."

"When can we have her back?" Pete glanced over at his wife.

"As soon as we've completed the forensic tests." She tilted her head. "You will have her back for a proper burial. I can't yet tell you when that will be, but we won't keep her any longer than necessary."

Her heart went out to the couple and she could see from the look on Dewi's face, and his glistening eyes, that his did too. Talking with a devastated family always brought home the terrible consequences of murder.

As they rose to leave, the DI placed a hand on Celia's shoulder to let her know she understood why Mrs Carter had remained silent and that it was okay.

～

The sun had dipped behind the clouds as they traversed the road to their car. They could see the remains of the castle in front and above them, and the sea off to their left.

They would now make their way further along the coast to Cardigan, and to the home of Victoria's father, Berwyn Mason.

∽

The cloud had mostly burned away as they parked their vehicle on the Main Street in Dolgellau.

Berwyn Mason lived alone, in a flat above a wool shop. His wife had passed away some years before, and he had never remarried.

He greeted them at the bottom of a flight of stairs that led directly to his front door.

The DI noted he walked with a limp.

At the time of his daughter's disappearance, Mason ran a successful business selling second-hand cars. He was currently unemployed. She wondered if losing his daughter was the reason he had given up the dealership.

"Berwyn Mason?" She asked, adjusting her face mask.

"That's me... Have you got ID?" He looked them over.

They flashed their warrant cards.

"Thank you, can't be too careful these days. Someone burgled a house up the road last month," he explained, leading them upstairs.

"Of course." Yvonne nodded. "But you know why we are here?"

"I know why you're here," he replied without turning round, as he unlocked the door.

It surprised her that he locked his flat when he was answering the outer door to the street. Perhaps the burglary up the road really had spooked him, but she wondered if he had other reasons.

They followed him through to the lounge of his two-bedroom home.

"Is your leg painful?" Yvonne asked.

He hitched his trousers up and adjusted his t-shirt before plopping down in fabric armchair that the DI was sure had seen better days, the floral pattern in it having faded to nebulous swirls.

Like many others suffering from the COVID lockdowns, he needed a decent haircut. The stubble on his face was almost a beard. "It has its moments," he replied.

"Arthritis?" She sat next to Dewi on the couch at right angles to Mason.

He nodded. "It's worse in the damp weather. It will ease a bit during the summer. Damn hip may need to be replaced. There's a long waiting list though, according to my consultant. At my age, I don't now if it's worth it." He sighed.

"I'm sorry about your daughter." She tilted her head. "I know the finding of her remains wouldn't have been the news you wanted."

"It wasn't," he agreed. "But it was hardly unexpected. I knew... I knew when they didn't meet Pete at the car, that something terrible had happened. They weren't the types to run off or not let us know they had changed their plans. Vicky would never have worried us. Bronwen, that was my wife, was convinced they were being held somewhere against their will, and believed they were still alive, even until she herself passed away from lung cancer. She kept telling me police would find them or that the girls would escape from their kidnappers. She thought sex-traffickers had taken them. I guess I always knew they would never come home. Somehow, I could feel they were dead. I could feel it in my bones."

Yvonne nodded. "We are investigating all avenues for what might have happened to Victoria and Helen. We need your help with understanding who they were and who their closest associates were."

"I'll do what I can."

"We read through the statements given by yourself, and other friends and family members. There was no mention of anyone bothering the girls. Do you remember if Vicky had concerns about people she knew? Did she ever worry that someone was stalking either herself or Helen, for instance? Even if she only talked about something in passing, it could be significant."

He frowned, shaking his head. "I thought it was more likely that they ran into someone at the festival. A stranger. And, no... Vicky didn't mention any such worries to me, and I think she would have done if something had scared her."

"I see, so you don't think anyone she knew would have followed her to the festival?"

"I can't think of anybody who might have done that." He grimaced. "I'm not ruling it out, I just don't think it likely. Vicky didn't say she was concerned and, if she had told her mum, Bronwen would have passed it on to me. I would have dealt with it. My wife and I didn't keep secrets from each other. I would have known."

"Berwyn...Were you named after the mountain?" Dewi asked.

Mason nodded. "My parents conceived me in the Berwyn Hills. My mother was Welsh and my father, English. They met on a hiking holiday in the region. I became a twinkle in my mother's eye on their first anniversary trip back there."

Dewi grinned. "That is a great story."

Mason pulled a face. "My parents were romantics."

"What was Vicky like?" Yvonne asked, leaning back on the sofa.

"Conscientious." He sighed, rubbing his forehead. "Kind, full of life, loving... She was a lovely girl. Not a day goes by without me thinking about her, and the life she could have had. She had a bright future ahead of her... They both did. I have missed her every day since that summer. But their lives weren't worth beans to whoever buried them out there in that wood. Their killer doesn't deserve the air he breathes. What gave him the right to take away their lives? I have always wondered how their killer could live with himself, but I bet he never gave them another thought."

The DI pursed her lips. "Their killer, or killers, will give them a lot of thought now. I should think they are having a few sleepless nights of their own."

"People like that don't have a conscience... I bet nothing disturbs their sleep."

"Well, we intend to inhabit their nightmares." She pressed her lips together, underlining her determination.

Dewi concurred. "They'll know we are going all out to find them. Trust me, they'll be losing sleep, just as you did when your girls didn't come home."

Mason tutted. "It doesn't matter what happens to them, they will never know or feel our pain. When I think of what my poor Bronny went through... She spent months waiting up every night, always checking her phone. It drove her to an early grave. I blame her illness on Vicky's killer. We were none of us the same after, Pete and Celia included."

"Did you see them much, after what happened?"

"Not as much, no. We'd known them for years, even

before the girls disappeared, Bronny and Celia took them to pre-school together. That's when we all lived in Dolgellau. Then they went to the same primary school. Those were the happiest days."

"You ran a business back then, what happened?" She tucked a lock of stray hair behind her ear.

"I let everything slide after Vicky vanished. It took the best part of ten years for the business to go under, but it was on a downward slope pretty much from the day she went missing. My mind wasn't on it, and the customers began slipping away."

"You mean the buyers for your vehicles?"

"Yes, I used to pride myself on the fact that my customers always returned when they wanted to change their car. But when I stopped paying attention, I lost them to other dealerships. You snooze, you lose."

"I see." She nodded. "I think most people would have struggled under the circumstances, Berwyn. You did well to keep it going as long as you did."

"It always happens to someone else, doesn't it? Until one day, it's you on the other receiving end of horrible news."

Yvonne thought of her husband and father, and her eyes glazed. "Yes…"

∽

As they left Mason's home, the DI thought about Guy Davies, and his mother, whose grief was still so fresh. She checked her watch; it was time to catch up with that investigation.

With two ongoing murder enquiries, her team word be working all hours for the foreseeable future. She would explain this to Tasha when she got home.

7

WHITE TRANSIT

That someone had abducted and murdered Guy Davies was obvious. What was not yet clear was why?

A public appeal for witnesses had so far yielded nothing. Somehow, a killer took a bound and struggling man up to the cliffs at Aberystwyth and threw him off.

"It would have taken two people," she said to Dewi the falling morning.

"I agree, it could be at a gang. Toxicology have confirmed there were no intoxicants in his system, not even alcohol. He would have been conscious, terrified, and fighting for his life."

She nodded. "But no-one saw them take him up the cliff. They're like ghosts."

Dewi had pushed his hands deep in his pockets, pondering this, when Dai Clayton caught up with them, looking pleased with himself.

"We have CCTV footage of a white transit van being driven up the back road to Constitution Hill at the time Hanson reckons the Guy Davies died. The van parked just after four-thirty am and is stationary for thirty-three minutes before it drives away again."

"Really?" Yvonne tossed her coat down on her desk. "Is anyone seen leaving the van?"

"No, ma'am. They exited on the opposite side from the camera. We have part of the vehicle in the frame, and that's all."

"Does that mean we don't have a registration number?"

"I'm afraid so. It was still dark, and the CCTV is grainy. We only see one side of the van. It's not great, but it gives us something to work with, and an idea of what to look for. The chances of it not being involved is slim-to-none, I'd say."

"Excellent work. Do we have a model? It would give us an idea of the reg year."

"They're fairly certain of the make and model, and can narrow down the year of manufacture. Meanwhile, we are going to carry on trawling all CCTV footage to see if we can peg its route to and from the Hill."

"That's great. It would be good to get images of whoever is driving the van. Keep looking, you're doing superb work."

"Thank you, ma'am."

∼

LATER THAT EVENING, an exhausted Yvonne returned home to find Tasha reading in front of the fire, an empty glass perched on the cream rug next to her.

The DI threw down her bag and joined her partner on the mat. "Have you eaten?" she asked.

Tasha shook her head. "No, I thought I would wait for my errant fiancé. I've made a tuna pasta bake. It just needs warming through and it is good to go."

Yvonne grinned. "You know that you're amazing... And I hadn't realised how hungry I was until now."

"Busy day?" Tasha leaned back, palms on the rug behind her, legs stretched out in front, wearing a sweatshirt and leggings.

The DI envied her relaxed state. "We have a couple of murder investigations running. We're stretched to the limit. The case is one from twenty-one years ago. A double murder. The other, happened last week. Someone tied a man up and pushed him off Constitution Hill in Aberystwyth."

Tasha winced. "I saw something about the clifftop case on the news and guessed your team would be investigating. Want to tell me about it?"

"We think they ferried him to the hill in a white transit. We're trying to identify and locate it."

"What about the other case?" Tasha tilted her head, examining the tired face of her partner.

Yvonne sighed. "You'll probably have seen that one on the news, too. Two sets of female remains found in Warren Wood. We think their abductor killed them soon after he took them from a summer music festival. We have very little to go on. Decomposition had completed, leaving only the bones and remnants of clothing. So perpetrator DNA is out of the window and finding the cause of death isn't easy, either. Our major piece of evidence is an old photo, showing the girls dancing while surrounded by a group who were staring at them."

"Are they your suspects?"

The DI hugged her knees. "They are on the list, yes. Unfortunately, we don't have the identities of all of those in the image. We know who the photographer is, and who two of the men are as they identified themselves previously. But the others are unknown, mostly because their faces are not as clear, or they are not facing the camera. I am surprised that the original investigation didn't chase them harder. Although, to be fair to them, it was only a missing person enquiry back then."

Tasha shrugged."It's different now, it's a murder investigation. You may find more people willing to come forward."

"I hope so. We must find them, Tasha. One or more of them could be the girls' murderer."

The psychologist rose from the rug, heading for the kitchen to reheat the pasta. "Is there any way that I can help?" she called. "Have a think, I'll be back in a minute."

The DI watched her leave with that relaxed walk of hers.

"Well?" Tasha asked, returning with their food which they began tucking into, still sat on the rug.

"Your help could be very useful love, but I think we need to know more about the backgrounds of these crimes before we'll have enough for you to work with. I still need to know who Guy Davies was. I'm due to have a chat with his mother in the next couple of days."

"Well, the offer is there, when you feel the time is right."

"Thank you, I appreciate it, Tasha."

~

He had been to this place many times since he was a boy. The area was a much-loved beauty spot, set in a rolling landscape with far-reaching views. Vivid greens hills faded to blue and purple in the distance. A vast and gentle lake set in one of the most idyllic valleys in Wales.

But not today.

The sun had disappeared behind a thick pall of cloud, leaving the vast stone edifice of Rhayader dam charcoal, sentinel and oppressive.

Simon Wells shivered at the sight of water spilling over the wall, fighting with itself. Clouds of spray and spiralling vortexes whirled in the mass below his feet.

He tugged at the ties around his wrists, desperate to wrest his hands from them. His bonds bit in, chafing the skin until he bled, refusing to give even a few millimetres.

Layers of duct tape muffled his cries, the sound barely audible above the roar of cascading water that would take him down, exchanging itself for the life-giving air in his lungs.

The wind buffeted the beleaguered man as his killers lingered out the minutes before death, torturing him with the knowledge of impending horror.

He tried shouting, "Get it over with!"

The stifled utterance went unnoticed. Hot tears wended their way down his face.

His tormentors said nothing, merely holding him by the elbows to keep him in place. Attired in black clothing and face masks, they appeared like devils, demons from another world.

Again muffled attempts to reason with them. "Why are you doing this? What have I done?"

His legs buckled and he would have fallen were it not for steely fingers sinking into his arms.

"Please, can't we talk about this?"

The crescendo of water drowned the scream as his body flip-flopped down the wall of the dam.

The killers watched the swell do their dirty work, walking away only when satisfied their victim struggled no more.

8

SENSELESS WASTE

Mrs Martha Davies held out a hand. Dark circles surrounded her azure eyes, and concave cheeks gave her an eerie appearance. She had lost weight, even since the last time the DI had seen her. Yvonne estimated about ten pounds.

Although COVID rules recommended otherwise, the DI accepted the offered hand. Those in Martha's age group had already received their vaccine, so the only risk was to the DI who had not. In Yvonne's mind, the mother's need for human kindness outweighed any concerns the detective had for her own safety.

A gentle squeeze for reassurance, and Yvonne broke the contact. "How are you, Mrs Davies?" She tilted her head, forehead lined in concern.

"I miss him..." Martha ran a hand through her shoulder-length silver hair. "I keep hearing footsteps approaching the back door and expect him to walk through it like he always did. Even though he had his own place, he still spent a lot of time at mine. Loved his home-cooked food, see."

"I'm sure he loved his mum, too."

"Yes." She gave a wistful smile, her eyes glazing over.

"What was he like, Mrs Davies? Who were his friends?"

"He was bright, funny, into everything, always active, and hungry. Guy was larger than life, but as honest as they come. My boy was a credit to me, and good to his friends."

"Did he have enemies? Anyone he was afraid of?"

Martha shook her head. "Guy was never one to mix with poor company. He was in the top set in school and did a diploma in finance at college. My boy was working in Town Planning for the council and enjoyed his job. He wasn't one to make enemies. People thought him firm but fair in his work. It was hard for anyone to get upset with Guy. He had a big smile and an even bigger heart. My son got on with everybody."

Yvonne made a few notes, after which she cast her eyes around the living room of the four-bedroom detached home on Mill Drive in Newtown.

Decorated in pale greens and beiges, Mrs Davies' small lounge was comfortable. She had amassed quite a collection of china dolls, which were kept in glass cabinets either side of the large bay window.

She brought her eyes back to Martha. "Was Guy different in the last few weeks before he disappeared? Was he out of sorts? Did he do anything he wouldn't normally have done?"

Mrs Davies shook her head. "Not that I could tell. The last time I saw him, he looked relaxed and happy. There was nothing different about him."

"When was that?" Yvonne tilted her head, tapping her pen against her lip.

"It was Thursday, the week before last, when he came by to return a book he had borrowed from me on French vineyards. He was due to go to the Dordogne this summer, but had to cancel his plans because of the pandemic. He changed his dates to later in the year." She sighed, a tear trickled down her cheek. "One of his secret ambitions was to own his own vineyard. There is one quite close to here. It's at the top of Newtown, just off the road past the hospital."

The DI nodded. "I know the one, but I've never sampled their wine."

"He would have been good at it." Mrs Davies continued. "He was good at everything he turned his mind to."

"I bet he was. His passing sounds a massive loss to the world, Mrs Davies."

"It is." Martha sighed. "Guy's friends feel lost without him."

"Who did he spend most time with?"

"I'd say Lisa, his girlfriend."

"Did they live together?" The DI paused her writing.

Mrs Davies shook her head. "No, he had lived with Ashleigh, his previous partner, but she moved out two years ago. He began dating Lisa last year."

"Were they happy together?"

"They had the occasional tiff, but who doesn't? They were only minor rows. I know they loved each other. Lisa was good for him. He went through a rough patch after the break-up with Ashleigh. Lisa helped him back to his feet, got him going out again. She had liked him for a while, but wouldn't have acted on it while he was with someone else. She's a nice person and came to see me a few days ago. We had a good cry together."

"Did Lisa have any jealous exes on the scene? Anyone who might have borne Guy a grudge?"

Mrs Davies shook her head. "Not that I know of... I think Guy would have mentioned it if there was."

"What's Lisa's surname? And how can I reach her?"

"Her last name is Thomas, and she works in the Black Boy, for Wetherspoons. She has a flat along the canal in Newtown."

"Did she ever stay at Guy's place?"

"She did, they were taking things slow and steady, otherwise she would have moved in."

"Thank you, Mrs Davies. Our forensic officers are going through your son's flat. It may be a week before you get his things." Yvonne rose from her seat. "In the meantime, if you think of anything I should know, please get in touch."

Martha nodded. "I will, Inspector. Thank you."

Yvonne gave her a reassuring smile. "We'll do whatever it takes to bring your son's killers to justice."

∼

Yvonne's pallor faded to the shade of her cream shirt as she listened to the call from Dewi.

"What's the matter? What is it?" Her partner scanned her face with concern, striding over to the DI and turning off the radio as she passed the sideboard in the lounge.

"I have to go, Tasha. They've found a body in Clywedog Dam."

"Why do you need to go? Is it murder?"

She nodded. "Someone tied the victim's hands behind his back. It could be a gang-related death."

"I see." The psychologist grabbed her partner's mac and helped her on with it. "Will you be back for food?"

Yvonne's face creased in apology. "I doubt it."

"It's okay." Tasha gave her a hug. "Just come back to me safely. I'll leave something in the fridge for you to pop in the microwave."

"Thank you." The DI grabbed her bag and checked her

watch. Four o'clock on a Saturday. Murder was antisocial in more ways than one.

~

DEWI MET her outside of the police station with the keys to an unmarked vehicle.

It took them forty minutes in the driving rain to arrive at the dam. Blackened skies rendered the countryside raw and bleak, the hills closing in against this thunderous backdrop.

The temperature had dropped a couple of degrees, leaving the DI wishing she had worn more than a thin mac over her skirt and blouse. She pulled her hands inside the sleeves of her coat.

Emergency service personnel thronged the roads along the dam. Paramedics, police, search and rescue personnel, crime scene investigators, and even firefighters were present. Flashing blue lights surrounded them all.

They caught up with a uniformed sergeant as he issued instructions to several junior officers from Llandrindod Wells station.

"Where is the victim?" Dewi asked him.

The sergeant pushed his hat back, wiping a hand over his brow and adjusting his face mask. "Down there." He pointed to a stretcher being carried by four men wearing search and rescue inflatable vests and red helmets, a few hundred yards below the road.

"Do we know who the victim is?" Yvonne asked, eyeing the bodybag on the stretcher.

The sergeant nodded. "We think it's Simon Wells. He's from Llandod and has been missing for nine days. His clothes matched the description of those Simon was last seen wearing. We've got people liaising with the family, to arrange for an identification."

She nodded. "We'll speak to Llandod officers."

"Poor sod." Dewi sighed. "I'll go down there and talk to search and rescue, get some details."

"Thanks." She gazed across the water. Two days of heavy rain had left water cascading over the walls, angry and beautiful. Her eyes closed as she thought of the victim, and the terror he would have felt at falling into the swirling waters, fighting to free his hands, unable to save himself.

"Are you all right, ma'am?" The uniformed sergeant was still there, his head tilted as he checked on her.

"Yes." She nodded, pushing the hood of her Mac off her head as the rain eased. "Is the pathologist on site? I haven't seen him."

He shook his head. "They're taking the body to the mortuary now, I believe."

"Right..." She continued to watch, as Dewi made his way back to her.

"They think he's been in the water at least a week." Her sergeant pulled a face. "He has massive head trauma, either before they threw him in, or from hitting his head on sides of the dam on the way down."

"Was he dead when he hit the water?" Yvonne frowned.

"They don't know. There was no frothing around the nose, but they can't say until they open up the lungs. It'll depend what Hanson finds. But, if he was still alive, it wouldn't have been for long, not in that torrent." He pointed to the threshing water at the base of the overflowing wall. "They think that is where he went in."

She nodded. "I thought it might have been. I'm worried about the escalation in gang activity in the area. This could be related. Maybe they punish members by throwing them in the water."

Dewi pursed his lips. "They're not making any attempt to hide the bodies. I mean, they didn't weigh him down at all."

"Could be a warning to others... Do as you're told or you'll end up like this."

Dewi checked his watch. "We'd better skedaddle, we've got Adrian Jones coming into the station at three."

Yvonne jerked into action. "God, I'd almost forgotten. Let's go."

9

FACES IN AN IMAGE

Yvonne's interviewee, Adrian Jones was one of the five men photographed as they watched Helen Carter and Victoria Mason dancing, prior to the girls vanishing from the AberFest music festival, in the summer of two-thousand.

Beside the photographer, the original investigation had only identified and questioned two of the five. Adrian, and Sam Evans who was due in to see her the following morning. They were two of the last people to see Helen and Victoria alive. If the team were to get to the bottom of what happened, the information they held could be vital.

The DI wanted to know who the unidentified men in the picture were and what they knew. They had never come forward, but they might talk now that investigators had found the remains of the girls. She hoped Jones and Evans could supply the identities that had eluded police for decades.

Jones attended the station ten minutes late, apologising profusely, until Yvonne held up her hand and told him to stop.

Forty-one-year-old Jones' suit trousers had creased, as though he had driven some distance before arriving. He'd loosened his shirt and tie and undone the buttons on his cuffs.

"Sorry, I drove from Llandrindod Wells." He looked at his watch.

She raised her right brow. "Llandrindod Wells?"

"Yes."

"Oh..." She checked her notes. "It says here, you manage a supermarket in Newtown, and that you were coming here straight from work."

He ran a hand through his close-cropped, dark hair. "I do, and I did, but I am helping to cover our Llandod store while that manager is off sick. There are never enough hours in the day. I got stuck in traffic, I should have been here half an hour ago."

"Don't worry about it." She led him through to the interview room. "Please, take a seat. We're waiting for Detective Sergeant Hughes to join us. What time do you have to be back?"

"Whatever time we finish." He shrugged. "I am in the Newtown store this afternoon until eight this evening. I can always finish a bit later to make up for lost time."

"Thank you for coming in, we won't keep you any longer than necessary."

As she seated herself opposite Jones, Dewi finally burst through the door.

"Sorry, ma'am." He nodded at the interviewee. "Mister Jones."

"Adrian, is it okay for me to call you that?" She began.

He nodded. "You can call me Adrian or AJ. I'm mostly known as AJ."

"AJ..." Yvonne perused her notes. "We have asked you

here today, to discuss two young women who disappeared twenty-one years ago, and whose remains we discovered in Warren Wood three weeks ago."

"Yes, the officer who spoke to me on the phone explained."

"I understand you were interviewed by police after the girls vanished. Do you remember that?"

"I do... It's a long time ago, though." He frowned. "I can barely remember."

"I have your statement here, AJ, if it helps?"

He swallowed, eyes wide.

"Would you like to see it? Jog your memory?" She slid a copy of Wyatt's photograph towards him. "It was a hot day. You were one of several people watching the girls dance at the time the photographer took this picture."

He peered at the photo. "May I?" He asked.

She nodded.

Jones picked it up, his eyes flicking between the faces. "I remember the festival, but I might be hazy about specifics. I mean, I met a lot of people that weekend, and it was twenty years ago."

"Of course, just try to remember what you can. Do you recall watching the women?"

"I do..." He chewed his bottom lip. "I remember their dancing was getting a lot of attention. They were throwing their arms and legs around and had accidentally hit a few people, spilling their drinks, you know. They were wild."

"How long were you watching?"

"Er... only a few minutes, I'd say. I mean, a photograph like that, well, it makes it look like I was having a good gawk for ages, but I really wasn't. They caught my attention for only a brief time."

"What were you doing for work back then? Were you employed?"

"I told officers I was claiming income support because I'd finished school and was about to start a plumbing apprenticeship with a local firm. In the meantime, I had two months before it started. I claimed benefit until I could earn a wage."

"Plumbing?" She tilted her head.

"I didn't go through with it." He looked at his hands on the table. "Plumbing wasn't really my bag. I wanted to work in a shop, so I applied for a job in a high street store in Newtown and got it. I had to let my dad down gently, plumbing had been his idea, you see."

"So, you were free during the time the festival was on?"

"Free?" He frowned.

"Yes, I meant there were no time constraints on you."

"My time was my own, yes."

"Did you travel to the festival alone? Or with others?"

"I travelled there alone. My uncle let me borrow his car. I bought a two-man tent, and off I went."

"How old were you?"

"Eighteen, you can work that out from my date of birth."

"What car were you driving?"

"An old Escort, I think. Blue. Made a lot of noise, if I recall rightly. People knew when it was coming."

"You borrowed the car a lot?"

"Yeah, I guess I did. I got a vehicle of my own the following year."

"Your uncle was kind, letting you drive his car like that."

He nodded. "I used to do odd jobs for him, you know, a bit of gardening or window cleaning. And I aways returned it in a cleaner state than it was in when I borrowed it. I would fill it up with petrol for him, too."

"Was your uncle at the festival?" She leaned back in her chair.

He shook his head. "No, he wasn't into live music."

"Did you bump into friends while you were there?"

"At the festival?"

"Yes."

"One or two, I stopped to say hello, but I didn't hang out with any of them."

"Why not?"

"They weren't close friends or anything."

"I see." She tapped the photograph. "So, tell me about the girls. You were there, an eighteen-year-old, out having a good time. You saw Helen and Victoria threshing about. Did you speak to them? Interact with them? Did you find them attractive?"

He lifted his eyes to the ceiling as he recalled the details. "I remember I saw the crowd parting, making way for something. That's what caught my eye first. I wondered what was happening. I thought maybe a fight had broken out, and I was wary as I didn't want to get caught up in anything."

"I see, and when did you realise it was the two women?"

"Almost straight away. I saw them throwing themselves around and realised they were probably drunk."

"Had you ever seen them before? Maybe earlier?"

He shook his head.

"Other witnesses said they saw the girls drinking lager, but not anything stronger. Did you see what they were drinking?"

"I would agree with the others. I saw one girl pour from a can into a plastic pint glass."

"Were they smoking? Or using anything?"

"You mean drugs? Not to my knowledge, but I really wasn't watching for very long."

"Did you?"

"Did I what?"

"Use drugs?"

"Me?" He frowned. "No."

"What happened next?"

"The girls became... they were really intoxicated... falling over, crashing into others, etcetera. One girl, the blonde one, fell to her knees and had to be helped up by the darker one, who began pulling her toward the toilets. Or, at least, that is where I assumed they were going. There were Portaloos at the edge of the field. They had to push through the crowds to get to them. They wouldn't have found that easy in the state they were in. I thought about offering my help, but... well... I felt shy. Being a quiet teenager, I was scared of girls. My fear of rejection stopped me from approaching them."

"Did you see anyone else offering help? Or talking to them?"

"Not for longer than a moment."

"Explain?"

"Well, twice, when the blonde girl-"

"Victoria."

"Victoria... When she fell, others stepped forward to offer their hands, but the dark one-"

"Helen."

"Helen lifted Victoria by herself."

"So you got the impression the girls were cautious around strangers?"

He nodded. "It seemed so. Like I said, they disappeared through the crowds, and I didn't see them again until their photographs appeared on the television because they were missing. I recognised them right away."

"You went to the police."

"Yes, they put this photo in the appeal." He pointed to Wyatt's picture. "And I saw myself. They said that the people in the photograph could help with enquiries. I handed myself in, because I wanted them to know I had nothing to do with the girls' disappearance."

"I see. Did you know any of the other men in the photo?" She pushed it towards him. "Have a good look."

He picked it up. "No." He shook his head. "I don't recognise anyone else. If I had, I would have told the inquiry a long time ago."

"What about the photographer, Andrew Wyatt, did you know him?"

"No, I'd never met him before. I couldn't even have told you his name, although I think I may have known it at one time."

"Did you speak to one another?"

"At the event? I can't remember."

The DI leaned forward. "Did you speak to him afterwards?"

"I saw him at the police station, weeks later."

"Why were you at the police station at the same time?"

He shrugged. "I don't think we should have been. I was late, and he was early for an interview. We bumped into each other in the carpark. I mean, no-one told us we couldn't talk to each other or anything. But, I felt uncomfortable, and I tried to walk away when he came over to my car. He followed me and continued making small talk. We weren't doing anything wrong, were we?" His eyebrows lifted with the inflection.

"It's not best practice for witnesses to confer on a case prior to interview. You should have realised that, since you were two of the last people to see the girls, you would have been on the suspect list, in the event the girls were harmed?"

He sighed, leaning back and folding his arms. "Well, I really didn't think that anything bad had happened to them at the festival. Everyone was having such a good time. I didn't suspect foul-play."

"What did you think might have happened?"

"Two young girls? Away from mom and dad? Beautiful weather? Alcohol and young men everywhere? I thought they had probably gone off for a few weeks, maybe gone travelling for a bit."

"Really?" She raised a brow.

"Look, I was young and naïve, okay? It's not what I would think these days. Back then, I trusted everyone. Kidnap and murder were the last things that sprang to mind. And people run away, don't they? I was sorry when I heard you had found their remains. They did not deserve that," he finished.

"Hmm..." Yvonne leaned back in her chair, scrutinising his face. "We may need to speak with you again, what's the best number to reach you on?"

"My mobile." He reached for her pen and notepaper. "May I?"

"Sure." She pushed it towards him.

He scribbled his number, adding an address for good measure. "You can reach me on that number, anytime."

"Thanks." She saw him out, her mind racing. Andrew Wyatt had not mentioned knowing Adrian Jones, or that they had chatted together during the previous investigation. The knowledge left her with a niggling feeling. She would moot it when she saw Wyatt again.

∽

THE ONLY OTHER person identified in Wyatt's photograph had been a young man called Sam Evans.

As Yvonne read through the file, she discovered they had interviewed him twice during the original inquiry. His statement held nothing out of the ordinary, but she wondered if DI Langford suspected Evans and, if so, why?

She renewed her determination to speak to the former detective, asking Callum to find his number.

In the meantime, Evans was due in to speak to her that afternoon. She would form her own opinions before seeking those of Langford.

Samuel John Evans, a county council employee, attended the interview on time. He appeared relaxed as he sauntered into the interview in a blue cotton shirt, open at the neck, and jeans.

He gave his date of birth as November twelve, nineteen-eighty, which would have made him nineteen at the time of Helen and Victoria's disappearance.

His light brown hair, neatly trimmed, was short in style and he had a light tan which appeared real. A small scar above his left eye was the only remarkable feature.

Dewi joined Yvonne, happy for her to take the lead.

Perversely, she felt a desire to rattle the self-assured man in front of her and mentally chided herself for this. Why shouldn't he feel confident? It might not be his fault that he became embroiled in a missing person enquiry and, subsequently, a murder investigation. Unless, of course, he was the architect of the girls' demise.

She cleared her throat. "Thank you for attending, Mister Evans, would you prefer Sam or Samuel?"

"Sam."

She nodded. "Very well, Sam. Do you know we have asked you here?"

"I was told it was because you found the remains of the girls that went missing twenty years ago."

"Twenty-one years, that's right."

The DI told herself that correcting him was necessary. It was right to be exact. But there was something about his straight back, level gaze, and piercing eyes that had her on edge. She thought he was weighing her up, getting the measure of her and probing for weak spots. "Did it come as a shock to you?"

"Do you mean their disappearance? Or the fact they turned up dead?" Evans fiddled with his left cufflink, turning it round and round.

"Both... Either."

"I'm not sure their disappearance surprised me."

"Why not?" She tilted her head.

He rubbed his forehead. "There was just something about the girls that day. I thought their behaviour risky. They were attracting a lot of attention and, along with their level of intoxication, that made them vulnerable. You never know who you might come across at an open-air event. Some people are not nice, as I'm sure you know better than most. Besides, I felt they had taken off for a few weeks as a sort of rebellion. Obviously, when they didn't return, my feelings on the subject changed. I felt relieved when police dredged the river and the girls weren't there. Some thought they might have had an accident in the sea later that night, but I always felt that something bad had happened to them in the fields. They were just so out of it."

"I see. Were you at the festival with others? Friends?"

He nodded. "I had agreed to meet up with friends — a couple. I hung out with them for most of the time, but they weren't with me when I saw the girls dancing. They were at the other end of the field and didn't see either of the young ladies."

"Did you notice whether the girls used substances? Or drank alcohol? Did they smoke?"

He shook his head. "I only saw Helen have a couple of swigs of lager, that's it. I would have said that Vicky was the more drunk of the two of them."

"Vicky?" She raised a brow.

"Yes."

"What made you call her Vicky? Were you on friendly terms with her?"

"No, but I watched the television appeals after their disappearance, and I remember her parents called her that. It stuck in my mind." He brushed his trouser legs as if ridding them of invisible crumbs.

"I see."

He jerked his head back, mouth falling open. "Oh, of course... I am a suspect. One of the last to see them alive, and I just referred to one of them by their pet name. I must be guilty."

"You would surely have been a suspect in their disappearance when detectives questioned you at the time, until they could rule you out?"

He shrugged. "I thought I was being helpful. I walked into the police station voluntarily."

"Did the girls acknowledge you in any way? Did they say hello?"

"No, they were way to engrossed in the music and lost in their drunken haze to pay me any heed. They were in a world of their own."

"How long were you watching them?"

"Oh, I don't know... ten or fifteen minutes?"

"Because they were attractive?"

He tilted his head, eyes piercing her. "Because of the spectacle they made." He sighed. "I don't find heavily intoxicated females attractive, I never did. I think people should be in control of themselves."

"So, you didn't approve if them letting their hair down?"

"I didn't say that. I thought they were going a bit too far with their crazy dancing and disruptive behaviour."

"And that is why you thought something bad might have happened to them?"

"Yes."

"Did you follow them through the crowd when they left to go to the toilets?"

He screwed up his face. "No, of course I didn't."

"Did you see anyone else follow them?"

"No, I didn't see them leave at all. I had turned my attention back to the stage by the time they left. I couldn't say whether they left with someone else."

"Just one more thing..." Yvonne rubbed her chin. "At festivals like this, isn't it considered normal to let go a bit? To get drunk and have a good time? It isn't an open invitation for someone to attack you."

He shrugged. "You should have been there. They really were going for it. I am not saying they were inviting an attack, I just think they could not take care of themselves in that state. You asked me if I'd seen them take anything. I didn't. But, if you were to ask me if I thought they might have, I would say yes. I think they had something in their system which was stronger than alcohol." He continued. "I have to go now, but you have my number if you need me. I am in the council offices nine to five, Monday to Friday."

"Thank you." She rose from her seat. "We may need to speak to you again. Detective Sergeant Hughes will see you out."

"What do you think?" She asked when Dewi returned.

"Honestly? I think he knows more than he's letting on."

She nodded. "I agree. For someone seemingly so self-assured, he fidgeted a lot."

"Are you still intending to speak to John Langford?"

"Yes, I know he's retired, but he appeared to be taking more than a passing interest in our Mister Evans, and I would like to know why. Technically, it was a missing person enquiry back then, but he interviewed Evans twice. There's nothing in the case file to say why."

"By the way, I meant to remind you it is Simon Wells' postmortem tomorrow afternoon. Are you going? Would you like me to go?"

"I'll go." She rubbed the back of her neck. "I'd like to see it for myself. The more I understand what happened to the victim, the more I'll know about his killer or killers."

"I still think it's two or more." Dewi pushed his hands into his trouser pockets.

She sighed. "I know, and that's all we need, a pair of killers. We're at full stretch. I shall have to request reinforcements at this rate. Whoever those killers are, we have to stop them."

"Right." Dewi nodded. "I had better get on. I've got Dai and Callum chasing down the rest of the unknown witnesses in that photograph. It's a long shot, but they're using facial recognition software, and comparing to the database. No luck so far, but you never know."

"I'll have my fingers crossed." She smiled. Steady and hardworking, her sergeant was the salt of the earth. "Thanks, Dewi."

10

WORD FROM THE WISE

Having retired from police work, former Detective Inspector John Langford had taken up bowls and gardening.

Yvonne agreed to meet him at his bowling club, in Newtown, where he played twice a week.

She found him in the bar, a plain rectangular room, decorated with trophies and photographs of past champions and championships.

Not everyone who drank there played the sport, the bar welcomed players, their friends, and anyone else who fancied tagging along. They also accommodated weddings, funeral wakes, and birthday bashes. All this added up to a much-loved venue, steeped in rich Newtonian history, with which its members regularly regaled those unfamiliar with the place. The DI knew this and prepared herself for keeping Langford on-point.

She entered and scanned the room. They had chosen a good time. It was quiet, save for the Motown playing in the background.

Beside herself and the barman, there were only three others, one of whom broke away to greet her.

"Yvonne Giles? John Langford, pleased to meet you. I would shake your hand, but..."

"I know." She grimaced. "These are strange times," she said, knowing he was referring to the pandemic.

There was a kindness and gravitas in his eyes, and life had lined his face with experience.

Yvonne felt calm in his presence. "Thank you for seeing me."

"It's no bother. It's nice to see someone new here, actually." He held his arm out in the direction of the bar. "Can I get you a drink?"

"An orange juice would be perfect, thank you." She reached for her purse.

"It's on me," he said, waving the bag away.

"If you're sure..."

"Give me a moment."

Her eyes wandered to the billboards outside, erected by local construction workers who were building something mysterious behind it. Perhaps she would ask Langford what they were up to.

He surprised her by using a walking stick as he returned with her drink, leaning on it as he passed her the orange juice. "Geoff will bring my pint over when it's ready," he explained, referring to the barman who was carefully pouring a Guinness.

"Are you okay?" she asked, eyeing the cane.

"Sciatica," he replied. "I've had it for a few months."

"Oh, I'm sorry. That must make bowling a little difficult?"

"It does, but I no longer play at county level, so I do the

best I can with it. Old age doesn't come by itself." He grinned.

"I hope this won't take too much of your time." She took out her notepad. "I wanted to discuss a cold case with you. You knew it as a missing person case. Helen-"

"Carter and Victoria Mason," he finished for her. "They vanished from a music festival."

"Yes, we found their remains in Warren Wood a few weeks ago. Someone murdered them around the time they disappeared, possibly while the festival was still in progress. The wood is very close to the field in which they were last seen."

Langford nodded, running his hand through thinning silver hair. "I think we let those girls down. We were understaffed at the time and, without bodies, we couldn't give the case the time it warranted. At least, I thought so. I was pretty sure someone had abducted them, but my superiors weren't happy about us spending so much time flogging a case when we couldn't even be sure whether they had run off somewhere. They wanted it dealt with as a missing person case, and that was that. I felt all along that it was murder."

"It must have been frustrating." She nodded.

"It was."

The barman placed Langford's drink on the table.

Yvonne scratched her head. "You said you suspected foul play, did you have a particular person in mind?"

Langford took a long sip of his Guinness, and licked the froth from his upper lip, taking on a thousand-yard stare. "There was no history of running away from home for either of the girls. Both had their university careers ahead of them and had no reason to disappear. We interviewed some of the festival-goers, and they all seemed to think the girls had gotten [become] too drunk. Some suspected a third person had spiked their drinks."

"I see... A similar thought crossed my mind. They went downhill rapidly, too rapidly for the amount of alcohol they were consuming. There is a photograph..."

"That's right, the one taken by an amateur who was there. We interviewed a few of those in that picture. The ones who had been watching the girls. I felt that one or more had to have seen something, but all of them denied having witnessed anything untoward taking place. We didn't get to speak to all of them, we couldn't identify everybody in the image. There were at least three we couldn't find. We issued an appeal, but they either didn't see it, or they didn't want to come forward."

"Maybe the abduction involved them?" She raised her eyebrow.

"Or they were uninterested," he agreed. "You want to identify them, anyway." He narrowed his eyes. "Of course it's suspicious that they made no contact, but you have to remember if we had found the bodies back then, those witnesses might have come forward. They probably didn't take the disappearance seriously. Missing people don't get the interest that murder victims do, unless it is a child of course."

"I know." She sipped her orange juice. "If we could find the last three witnesses in that photograph, we might have the pieces of the puzzle we are missing."

He nodded. "It's possible. Did you talk to the photographer?"

"I did. He couldn't tell me who the others were in the photo either, though he also failed to tell me he had talked to one of them in the carpark before you interviewed them. Apparently, he and AJ had chatted."

"Well, I didn't know that." Langford frowned.

"Hmm..." She sipped her juice. "AJ told me that Wyatt's attention made him uncomfortable."

"Neither of them mentioned it to me."

Yvonne leaned in. "Did you have a suspect in mind? Someone who stood out for you?"

He pursed his lips, his gaze turning to the window. "I suspected a guy called Sam. I forget his last name..."

"Evans, I've met him." She nodded. "I spoke to him the other day."

"Yes, well, a rumour circulated that he was showing a great deal of interest in the case. Someone suggested he had changed his t-shirt in the middle of the afternoon on the day the girls vanished. We couldn't verify that, but we got a warrant to search his room. His clothing tested negative for blood. However, we found cuttings from newspapers covering the story of the missing women. It looked like he had bought a copy of every single newspaper and magazine that had covered the story, and cut out the articles. He had literally amassed piles of publications, and he had cut only one story out from each."

"Was he pasting them in a scrapbook?"

Langford shook his head. "No, he put them in a shoebox which he stored in the bottom of his wardrobe."

"What did he say when you questioned him about it?"

"He said he kept them because he'd been at the festival, and he felt invested in the case. He said he only wanted to help, like he imagined himself as an amateur detective."

Yvonne frowned. "He didn't mention the shoebox to me, or wanting to help solve the case, but then you never mentioned it in the original case file, either." She searched Langford's face. "Why did you leave it out?"

He sighed. "Same reasons I gave you. We had no bodies

and no proof of foul play. Evans employed a solicitor who got an injunction against us holding that information in the file, because we had nothing to suggest a murder had taken place. The girls may simply have gotten so intoxicated, they had a mishap somewhere, possibly in water, and died. His solicitor convinced a judge that Evans was merely a mysteries enthusiast, fascinated by the girls' disappearance, which he certainly was. I thought him obsessed. But, I had nothing concrete to suggest he was any more involved than that."

"Well, that old injunction won't protect him now." She pressed her lips into a line.

"Quite right," Langford agreed.

"Anyone else you think I should look at?" she asked, searching his face.

"There was no-one else who piqued our interest as much as Evans. We had to put the case in cold storage, but you have the bodies. You can go after him."

She nodded. "Oh, I intend to."

∽

"It would fit..." Dewi placed his hands on his hips, pondering the previous investigator's information. "He keeps a crazy amount of newspaper cuttings and injects himself into the case early on. But, John Langford put the frighteners on him by getting too close."

Yvonne perched on the edge of her desk. "Yes, but we should remember that he didn't present to police until after they launched the appeal for the men in the photograph. So, technically, he had a legitimate reason to come forward."

"But why then does he get his solicitor to file for an injunction to stop Langford's team keeping information on him. That doesn't sit right with me. I mean, if he's innocent, why do that?"

"Exactly, I'm going to talk to him again."

"Want me with you?"

"I do, Dewi. He'll be here in the morning. Let's see how he answers our questions. It's a whole different ball game, now we have the remains."

"You bet."

"Have got anything back from forensics?"

"They think Helen died from strangulation. Victoria's cause of death is unknown. They've warned that we may not get an answer for how she died, Yvonne."

She nodded. "We'll see what Evans has to say for himself."

11

PRIME SUSPECT?

Evans presented in a shirt and tie, matching tie-pin and cufflinks, and shiny shoes.

The DI got the feeling he had bought his footwear especially for the interview.

"Sam, thank you for coming back in at such short notice," she began.

He stared at her, scouring her face as though to glean her thoughts. "I must admit, you surprised me."

She nodded. "I'm sure. I wanted to ask you about the newspaper cuttings you kept of Helen and Victoria's disappearance. DI John Langford explained to me that you kept a considerable number in a shoebox. Is that correct?"

His face flushed. Eyes, almost black, bored into her. "There's an injunction against that information being used."

"No," She shook her head. "That ruling applied only because there was no evidence of murder. We are in a whole new scenario, now. We know someone killed the girls and buried them."

"Are you going to arrest me?"

"Did you murder Helen and Victoria?"

"No, of course I didn't."

"Do you want your solicitor with you?"

He shrugged. "It was just cuttings." He stretched his legs out under the table, crossing them at the ankles. "I was as keen as anyone else to know what happened, because I saw them that day, and I felt like I knew them."

"But you didn't talk to them, according to your statements, so what made you feel you knew them at all? It seems an odd thing to say."

"All right, I saw them, whatever, it was enough to make me interested in what had happened, and to help find them."

"Tell me about the injunction."

He narrowed his eyes. "Why?"

"Because, you said you wanted to help with the investigation, and yet you put up barriers, preventing police from doing their job."

"Look, back in the day, if police questioned you, you were as good as guilty in the eyes of the public, even if they later found you to be innocent. People would still say there was no smoke without fire. It could ruin a person's reputation, their career, and relationship prospects. If they would not arrest and charge me with something, I didn't see that they had a right to keep information about me." He glowered at her. "It isn't a crime to care."

"Did you suspect anyone at the time?" she asked, looking to calm him down.

"No, I told you, I didn't know who might have hurt the girls. It was my father who organised the solicitor and the injunction, not me. I was young, and I didn't have a clue why there was so much fuss about the clippings. I was a teenager, for goodness' sake."

Her voice softened. "The last thing I want is for an

innocent person to have their name or reputation tarnished. I don't wish to hang this crime on anyone who isn't guilty of it. Trust me, this case will have due process. When we bring the perpetrator or perpetrators to justice, and we will, we'll do it on irrefutable evidence, not suspicion and rumour."

He sighed, the tension in his posture easing. "Well, that is a relief, Inspector."

∼

Hanson let her into the floodlit mortuary where Simon Wells lay, under a plain white sheet, on a metal trolley.

Since he was the second victim found bound and thrown to his death, Yvonne had a good idea of how extensive his injuries would be.

"I'll be with you in a moment," Hanson called. "Just need a couple of minutes."

"No problem." She looked at the clock. "I've got about an hour."

"Oh, thank goodness." His face relaxed. "I had to collect my son from school. He's unwell, and now he has to self-isolate. My wife couldn't get away in time to pick him up."

The DI nodded. "I understand, we live in crazy times. Is he all right?"

"At fifteen, he feels he can look after himself, but my wife has taken time off to keep an eye on him." He pulled back the sheet, exposing the head and upper torso of the dead man. The victim lay pale and cold on the surface. The DI could see for the first time how he might have looked in life, minus the facial bloating that had occurred. Between his red-brown hair and beard, freckles peppered his nose and the tops of his cheeks.

"Port-wine birthmark." Hanson turned the victim's head with his gloved hand.

She peered over the pathologist's shoulder.

Simon Wells' beard covered all but the top portion of the stain on his right cheek, but as Hanson parted the hairs, they could see that the purple birthmark covered approximately one square inch of skin, and was shaped like the country of France. The pathologist took a photograph.

"Shall we begin?" he asked.

"I'm ready when you are." Yvonne closed her eyes for the first incision, something she always did. For her, it was that hardest thing to watch, that breaking of the skin. She opened them again when she realised he was beginning with the injuries to the head.

"We have a four-inch laceration to the scalp on the right-hand side," he began. "And bruising consistent with a glancing blow, possibly sustained as his head struck the wall of the dam on the way down."

"He fell head-first?"

"I would say so. He may have flipped over when he struck the wall, but I think they threw him head-down."

"Could that injury have killed him?"

"It's possible, but I won't know for sure until I examine the lungs. What I can say, is that it likely rendered the victim unconscious. He would have been unaware of hitting the water."

"Small mercies..." Yvonne sighed. "At least he didn't suffer for too long."

"No," Hanson agreed. "He wouldn't have known he was drowning even if he was alive when he hit the water."

"Have we had the toxicology results back yet? Was there anything in his system?"

Hanson grabbed his scalpel. "No, I sent blood and hair

for analysis, and they came back negative. I can't rule out something like GHB, because of the speed it goes out of the system, but we found nothing in the samples. He wasn't under the influence when he died."

"Okay." She averted her gaze as the surgical blade did its work, her thoughts turning to the person or persons who had killed him.

Hanson excised and weighed organs, collecting samples as and when. "There's water present in the lungs, consistent with drowning. We'll compare it with water samples from the reservoir to confirm that's where he drowned."

Yvonne ran her eyes over the dead man. "It doesn't look like they beat him."

"That's right," Hanson agreed. "Everything I've found so far is consistent with being restrained and thrown off the reservoir wall. I think he died around forty-eight hours after they abducted him."

"Maybe they waited until they thought no-one would see them."

The pathologist nodded. "And the pandemic lockdown may have given them greater opportunity for cover."

"Perhaps we have serial killers who are taking full advantage of the lack of people at these beauty spots."

"I'll let you know the results from the samples when we get them back."

"Thanks, Roger." Her shoulders sagged as she left the mortuary. The second murder in a matter of weeks. God only knew if they had enough time to prevent the next.

12

MIND BLOWN

"Any news on the white van seen in Aberystwyth?" she asked Dewi, catching up with him in the station the following morning.

He shook his head. "Uniform have been up and down the streets making enquiries, and we've checked possible local vans and ruled them out. To be honest, without a reg it's an impossible task. We have CCTV from around the town for the time of interest, but it will take us a while to go through it all."

"Keep on it." She pursed her lips. "These killers are like phantoms, and they seem to know the weak spots in the system. Check out the van-hire firms, too. The perpetrators may not be using their own vehicle. Have we got anything back from the digital lab regarding the victims' phones?"

"I'll get on to them, ma'am." He checked his watch. "Don't forget, you have Andrew Wyatt coming in at ten-thirty this morning for questioning over the remains in the wood."

"Yes, thank you, I hadn't forgotten."

WYATT ATTENDED ON TIME, in a casual shirt and jeans.

"Day off?" she asked, as they entered the interview room.

"Week off." He grinned. "I'd been planning to go away, but that's off the agenda with the COVID lockdown."

"At least we have better weather now." She placed her notes down on the table, showing him a seat. "Make the most of it."

He was watching her. She could feel his gaze like a physical entity invading her skin. "You're probably wondering why we asked you back in here again?"

He folded his arms, leaning back in his chair. "I was curious, yes. I thought I'd told you all I know, the last time we spoke?"

"You were helpful," she agreed. "However, I am left with one or two questions, now that I've spoken to some of those who were in your photograph. The one you took at the festival and handed in to police."

"Oh?" He leaned forward, unfolding his arms. "What questions?"

"Do you remember being interviewed by the original inquiry team?"

"Yes, didn't I tell you that last time?" He frowned.

"You did. You told me you thought your picture could be helpful to the investigation."

"Obviously."

"Had you any other motive for presenting yourself to the inquiry?"

"What do you mean?" His eyebrows dipped in the centre.

"It gave you access to other witnesses."

"What?" He crossed his arms.

"People travelled from all over Wales to be at that festival. That made them hard to trace. But if you hung around the incident room, you could bump into anyone who had information."

"What are you implying?"

"I'm suggesting you may have wanted to find out what others knew?"

"You think I might have offered my help because I carried out the abduction? Is that what you're saying?"

"Why would I be thinking that, Mister Wyatt?" She had him where she wanted him. "I'm merely suggesting that, as a young photographer, you might have been looking for an angle or a story, to go along with your picture. Something with which you could approach local newspapers."

His shoulders relaxed. He placed his palms down on the table. "I see."

"Did you speak to other witnesses at the time?"

He shrugged. "I don't think so."

"Think about it."

"I don't need to think about it, I didn't. And I wasn't looking for any story angle."

"Are you sure you didn't have a conversation with another witness, someone from your photograph?"

His nostrils flared. "I just said so, didn't I?"

"What about when you turned up for your second interview with DI John Langford? Not the one where you handed in your picture, but when he asked you back for formal questioning?"

"I can see you have something specific in mind, so I think you had better spit it out because I don't remember."

"We have a witness who asserts you spoke to him in the carpark, prior to that second interview."

"Am I allowed to know who?" He folded his arms again, pushing back his chair to stretch out his legs.

"In due course..." She was reluctant to name Jones in case it put him at risk. "Our witness states that you approached him in the carpark, asking him what he knew. It stuck in his mind. I think it made him uncomfortable."

"If I spoke to someone, it was just to be friendly. I would have been making conversation. We were probably feeling nervous."

"So you agree you talked to other witnesses?"

"Look, since when has chatting been a crime? They hadn't accused me of anything. They hadn't arrested me. There were no charges."

"The witness tried to walk away. He said he wanted to discourage you, but you pursued the conversation."

"Why didn't you just say that to me in the first place? And why didn't he just tell me he wasn't happy to talk? I'm not very good at guessing games, I'm afraid."

"Some people lack the confidence to speak their minds to others, particularly when the others in question have a more forceful personality. However, most of us can accurately read the body language of another and know when they are not interested, but you either didn't read the signs or actively ignored them."

Silence.

"Perhaps, he felt intimidated?"

"Intimidated? What?" He frowned. "Look, this is getting silly." He leaned in, his eyes were black. "We need to walk this back. I was not probing anyone for information, I was not trying to intimidate anyone, and I was not, repeat not, involved with whatever happened to those two young women. I didn't even get to speak to them. They caught my attention with their outrageous dancing. I took a photograph. That's all I did."

In that moment, she thought him capable of violence, instinctively moving herself back in her seat. If he was guilty, however, he was doing a good impression of righteous indignation.

"I had to ask you, Andrew," she said, hoping to de-escalate his heightened emotional state. "Can you remember what you discussed with the other witnesses?"

He shrugged. "I only spoke to one. I think his name was Jones. He looked nervous, come to think of it. I thought he looked shifty. He was all hunch-shouldered and kept looking down. He looked like he had something to hide."

"So you didn't think it was nervousness about talking to you?"

"That wasn't my impression."

"What did he say to you?"

"He said he hadn't been watching the girls for that long, and that he wasn't staring at them. Said my photo made him look like a creep. He knew about my picture, but I swear I wasn't the one who told him."

"He would have seen in it on the television, Andrew."

"They dropped the investigation not long after that, you know."

"They didn't drop the case." She fixed him with her gaze. "They just couldn't take it forward at the time as they hadn't found the bodies. This is a whole new ballgame, Andrew. We have the remains, and we have ways of making them talk, Mister Wyatt. We would like to take a DNA sample from you, is that okay?"

He grimaced. "I doubt you'll get useful DNA from their remains after they have been in the ground for two decades." He sighed. "I'm sorry, I didn't mean that the way it sounded. Yes, you can swab my DNA. Do you need a blood sample?"

She shook her head. "A cheek swab should suffice. We may ask for a blood sample at a later date, but only if we have a positive match."

"Which won't happen..."

The DI was quite happy to let him have the last word. In the meantime, she rang through to the office to request a DNA swab kit.

Dewi took the cheek swab, bagged it for the lab, then accompanied her back to the office after Wyatt departed. "He looked cheesed off. Do you think he has something to hide?"

"I can't quite work him out." She sighed. "One minute he is charming, and the next... He's volatile, Dewi, but as far as murdering the girls? I don't know. Perhaps he is hiding something, but we haven't found it yet."

Dewi nodded. "Oh, before I go, Dai was looking for you. He says he has information regarding Guy Davies' and Simon Wells' mobile phones."

"Right, thank you, Dewi."

∽

She caught up with Dai and Callum as they searched through CCTV footage for the white transit.

"Have you found anything?" She perched on the edge of Callum's desk.

"Not yet, we have a couple of registrations to check out, but I doubt either of them will be the one we want. I think our killers chose their times and places carefully, to evade cameras and prying eyes."

"Hmm..." She rubbed the back of her neck. "I hear you have information on the victims' mobile phones?"

"Ah, yes." Dai pulled out a sheaf of printouts. "Guy Davies's phone was in his jacket pocket. The digital lab pulled up all the text conversations and phone calls he made in the days leading up to his disappearance. It's all in here." Dai lifted the papers. "I've taken a cursory look, and I agree with the lab. There's nothing in there to suggest anyone would want him dead. There are no threats, no off conversations, not a nasty word. I thought you might like to look yourself, ma'am."

"Thank you, Dai. What about Simon Wells?"

"Ah..." He grimaced.

"What?" She raised a brow.

"They had to dry out both of the victims' phones in order to get the information off the chips."

"And?"

"And that worked for Guy's phone, but unfortunately, the chip in Simon's mobile bubbled."

"Meaning?"

"They couldn't pull anything off it, ma'am. We'll get some info from the phone company regarding numbers dialled etc, but the messages on the chip have gone."

"Oh, no..." She ran a hand through her hair.

Dai continued. "But if Guy Davies' phone is anything to go by, we might have gleaned nothing useful from it, anyway. It could have been just as innocuous as his."

"So, we have no link to drugs, or gangs. Nothing untoward."

Dai shook his head. "Nope."

"And, no difficulties with anyone."

"Right again. There's nothing there."

"Okay, we're back to the drawing board as regards a

motive. Keep digging both of you, you're doing an outstanding job."

Callum came from behind his desk, smoothing the creases in his trousers. "I need to stretch my legs." He grinned.

"I thought you'd given up?" The DI laughed.

"Oh, come on, ma'am, it's all these troublesome cases you give us. They drive me to smoke."

"Shouldn't that be driving you to drink?"

"That's later."

She chuckled. "Don't get bladdered. I need my top DCs on the ball."

"Top DCs? We're your only DCs."

She tossed her pen at him. "Go have your smoke. You can make a round of coffees when you get back for your cheek."

He laughed as he left. "My God, Yvonne, you drive a hard bargain."

She turned back to Dai. "Did the lab look at GPS data? Can they give us an idea of where Guy was when they abducted him? I know it's a lot to ask, but you could match anything significant to CCTV. That would be really helpful. I'd like to know who he met, and where. It's just possible that his kidnappers spoke to him some time before taking him. It's a long shot, but anything you get could make a difference."

"On it... leave it with me."

∼

DCI LLEWELYN strode through the door. "Yvonne... just the person."

"Chris."

"Could I have a word?"

Her heart sank. She had very little for him. "Yes, of course, sir."

He placed his hands deep in his pockets, his tie hung loose, and his hair needed a comb. "How's it going? Anything happening with the dead girls' case? I've had reporters and the crime commissioner on the phone wanting answers."

"We're interviewing witnesses from the time, and we have forensics and anthropology working with the remains. We're trying to piece everything together, but it's taking longer than usual because their memories are poor."

"What about Guy Davies and Simon Wells? Are those investigations moving forward?"

"We're analysing phone records and CCTV."

"Do you have suspects in either case?"

"We do in relation to the murdered girls, but the cases are weak. There's a lot still to do. We have no-one in the frame for killing the men. However, I believe the murders of the two males are linked because of the use of zip-ties to bind their hands, and the same type of duct tape was used to gag them. Not the same reel, though. They must have bought a new one. Unfortunately, water may have destroyed any DNA and fingertip evidence. We hope that when we find the van used to transport the victims, we'll get fibres and DNA from that. Forensically, that may be our best bet. I'm sorry, sir, I wish I could give you more."

He smiled. "It sounds like you have everything in hand. I know you'll get there. Keep going."

He walked off down the corridor, leaving the DI exhaling with relief.

As she travelled home that night, Yvonne thought of Guy and Simon, and the terror they would have felt at being abducted and knowing they were about to be thrown to their deaths.

She shuddered, perhaps it was similar for the two young women taken decades before. Perhaps they had also known what would happen to them. She wondered, not for the first time, how anyone could lack so much empathy with fellow human beings they could become a life-taking psychopath.

Welcoming lights were on outside her home as she turned into her drive shortly after nine-thirty. Tasha had left them on for her.

She smiled to herself. She couldn't wait to see her partner for some much-needed downtime.

The psychologist greeted her in the hall, taking her bag and coat.

It was precious, feeling cared for like that. The weight of everything fell away in that moment, like the relief you feel when a fever breaks and you know you're on the mend, or when you're in chronic discomfort, and the painkillers finally kick in. Yes, such love healed her from the gravity and weight of the day.

"Are you all right?" Tasha asked.

The DI hugged her, holding her tight. "I am now."

"Hard day?" The psychologist was already in her blue-striped PJs, a half-drunk mug of hot chocolate on the coffee table.

"You could say that." She nodded.

"I've left soup and fresh bread by the microwave. Are you ready for it?"

"I'll get cleaned up first, thank you." She rubbed tired eyes. "You make all the difference," she said, yawning.

"You get showered, I'll reheat your dinner." Tasha

rubbed her partner's cheek. "Go get comfortable. It's homemade chicken soup and sourdough bread I bought from the deli in town. It'll warm you through."

Yvonne hadn't realised how cold she had become. Though spring had well and truly sprung, and the day had been unseasonably warm, the nights were still frosty.

She lingered under the hot shower, allowing its warmth to penetrate her body. The water soothed her aching brain. Tomorrow would be a better day.

∽

AFTER CONSUMING Tasha's delicious soup, Yvonne sat with her on the cushions in front of the fire. "It was a tough day," she admitted.

"Want to talk about it?" The psychologist leaned against the foot of the sofa, stretching her legs out in front of her.

Yvonne, now also in PJs, adjusted the towel around her hair. "It's been a one step forward, two steps back sort of day."

"I saw a news special earlier about the girls in Warren Wood. I thought of you."

"What did they say?"

"They had a rushed interview with your DCI. They put him under pressure. I thought he handled it well. He told them you are making progress."

"Me?"

"He mentioned you and your team, yes."

"I wish it felt like we were. Wait..." The DI ran to the hall to retrieve a copy of Wyatt's photograph from her bag. "Look at this." She handed it to Tasha.

"What am I looking for?" she asked, scanning the image.

"Someone took it not long before the two girls disappeared. That was them dancing at the festival. We are working our way through the people who were watching, interviewing all of those we can trace."

"Including the person who took this photo?"

"Yes, why do you ask?"

"In case this photo was the killer's souvenir."

"Yes, I wondered if it could have been a trophy of sorts. The photographer volunteered it to the original missing persons inquiry."

"Wow." Tasha frowned. "The girls look out of it."

"I think they were." Yvonne nodded. "I think the killer may have spiked their drinks."

"Using what? Benzo's? GHB?"

"That's what I think. All they had to do was wait for it to take effect. Victoria succumbed first. She started falling into people and onto the floor. Helen was trying to help her to the toilets when witnesses last saw them. By then, Helen was also showing signs of being heavily intoxicated. That was the last time anyone admits to seeing them alive."

"I see..."

"There are three men in that photograph who never came forward. They didn't respond to the original request for information, and they have so far not been in touch with us either."

"Perhaps, they don't think they have anything useful to add."

"Maybe, but look," she pointed to their faces. "They are definitely watching, and surely wouldn't have forgotten that. Hang on..." The DI grabbed the photo, pulling it closer for a better look.

"What is it?"

Yvonne ran to the cabinet to grab a magnifying glass from the drawer.

"Yvonne?"

"That looks like..." Her mind wandered back to the recent postmortem.

"What?" Tasha frowned.

"I need this image blown up." She pointed to a bearded youngster in the image. "I think I viewed his body in the mortuary yesterday. I think this could be a young Simon Wells."

"Is that the guy they pulled out of a Rhayader dam last week?"

"It is."

"Do you have the original picture file? You may get better enhancement from that."

The DI shook her head. "The original inquiry only kept one physical photo. I don't think they ever had the original file."

"Can you get it?"

Yvonne nodded. "I can try. I'll ask Andrew Wyatt for it. He took the picture. Maybe he still has it. If that is a port-wine birthmark I see, in that beard, I'll know it's Simon."

"You could ask his family, they would recognise him."

Yvonne pursed her lips. "I will as a last resort. I don't want to go to grieving parents and explain that this photo connects their dead son to a decades-old double murder."

"Do you think there may be a link between the cold case and the new one?"

She rubbed her forehead. "I don't know. I hadn't linked them before, but Guy Davies was murdered two weeks after the girls' remains were found, and Simon Wells about a week after that. Wait..." Yvonne peered at the image again. "Perhaps Guy Davies is also in this image."

"But, if the killers murdered Guy and Simon, they must have thought they had seen something."

"Yes, and the murderer must have known their identities from the start."

"It sounds almost too far-fetched..." Tasha frowned.

Yvonne nodded. "The truth often does."

"How will you get the original picture file?"

"I'll phone Wyatt tomorrow. I'll say we need it to produce a poster to jog people's memories."

"There could be others on that photo who are in danger, if your suspicions are correct."

"I know. We'll have to move fast. Someone connected to that photograph knows far more than they have ever admitted. I'm going to interview all known witnesses again."

"Don't put yourself in danger, Yvonne."

"I won't, I promise."

13

OPEN AVENUES

"Can you get this blown up for me?" Yvonne passed the photograph to Callum the following morning. "I'm requesting the original from Andrew Wyatt, but in case we don't get it, see what you can do. I think this guy is Simon Wells." She tapped the bearded man in the image. "And this could be Guy Davies," she said, singling out another.

"Bloody hell!" Callum raised both brows.

"Bloody hell, indeed. If I'm right, it will blow our cases wide open."

"That's incredible..." Callum scratched his head. "You're saying it could be the same killers."

"Uh huh, and they're taking out the witnesses to their original murders."

"Wow." Callum shook his head. "Well, I never considered that..."

"I need the image, ASAP," she prompted.

"What? Oh, yes, I'm on it."

They cycled from vehicles left at opposite ends of town, one deposited at the Park and Ride on the Boulevard De Saint Brieuc, and the other at the church carpark near the Old College.

Leaning their bikes against the wall on the prom, they walked toward the beach, leaving their cycle helmets on.

The pandemic-induced lockdown was easing, and people were once again venturing into town, and onto the promenade.

The men were two of many making the most of this newfound freedom in the spring sunshine. It was the perfect cover for a clandestine meeting on the shale, metres from the sea.

"You left your phone at home?" The man in the grey helmet leaned back on his hands, the heels of which sank into the damp sand.

"Yeah, of course, what about you?" The guy in the red helmet cast his eyes both ways along the beach.

"Yep, just making sure we don't get tracked."

"Got it. So, what's the plan?"

"I've got another plate for the van."

"That was quick."

"It was. I paid for it, though. It cost me a ton."

"Does he know to keep his mouth shut?"

"He won't say anything and risk losing business. I trust him."

"Fair enough."

"This one's going to be tougher than the last. We'll need to keep it tight. There's few people living there, and the neighbours watch each other's properties."

"We'll have to be in and out."

"Exactly... And he doesn't go out much. Comes home from work, stays in, watches TV. That's it..."

"So, do we hit him after work?"

"We'll have to. Lucky for us, he gets back late, between eight and eight-thirty. If we do it within the next week, it'll be dark when we set off."

"Good."

"Yeah, I still have to figure out the best place to park the van."

The other man leaned forward, wincing as he did, clasping his hand to his right side.

"What's the matter?" grey hat barked. "You're not crying off?"

"No, of course not. I wouldn't do that. I'm just sore... caught an elbow in the ribs last time, and I think he cracked it. It's on the mend, but it hurts if I move too fast."

"You going to be fit for this take? We can't afford for anything to go wrong. It's getting a lot of attention. There are cops all over the place. We can't mess up."

"I'll be fit." Red hat rubbed his side. "Where are we lifting him from? Like you said, there's police everywhere."

"I've got the place. It's remote enough. We should be okay there after dark, providing I can find a somewhere to park the van. There's no CCTV. I might need some traffic cones, to block off part of the lay-by. We won't be there any longer than necessary."

"Are you going to tell me where it is?"

Grey hat shook his head. "You don't need to know until we're on the way there."

"Wait up," red cap warned.

Two beat officers walked the prom behind.

The riders leaned away from one another.

The officers paid them no heed.

"Everything we need will be in the van. Don't forget your balaclava, dark clothing, and leather gloves."

"What if he struggles?"

"You hit him."

"Me?"

"I'm bigger than you, I get the hood on. You hit him only if you need to. Got it?"

"Got it."

Grey cap sighed. "Don't fuck up. I'll slip an envelope in your *letter box and let you know where and when. Read it, memorise it, burn it."*

"Right."

"Make sure you burn it."

"I will."

"Don't bring your phone. No technology of any sort."

"Got it."

"And strap up that bloody rib."

14

CLEAR AS MUD

Callum pulled up the digitised photograph sent to him by the lab. "They've done a good job, ma'am, from what we sent them."

"Thank goodness." She had worried they wouldn't get a good enough reproduction, since Wyatt told them he deleted the file by accident when the original inquiry requested it from him.

She peered over Callum's shoulder, Dewi standing to her right.

They waited, holding their breath as Callum zoomed in on the bearded man.

"Can you go in more on the beard, Callum?"

"I can."

"Stop!" She leaned in, pointing. "Look, right there..."

They peered at the screen.

"Can you sharpen the image?"

"I can try."

Yvonne grinned. "Well done, Callum."

"Christ!" Dewi shook his head.

Yvonne ran a hand through her hair, her suspicion

confirmed. The bearded man in the photo had a France-shaped port-wine birthmark on his right cheek. "Do me a favour, Callum, cross-check this with the photographs taken of Simon Wells in the mortuary. Let's be absolutely certain we have this right."

"Would you like me to check the man we think is Guy Davies, too? I know we have less of his face, but we probably have enough."

"Get the lab to confirm the identification, Callum. This puts a whole new slant on our case. I'll let Llewelyn know, the minute the lab gets back to us."

"Right you are, ma'am."

"Excellent work, Callum."

"It was your idea, Yvonne."

She grinned. "I do all right, sometimes."

～

SHE STRAIGHTENED her skirt before giving the door two firm raps.

"Come in."

She shut it behind her.

"Ah, Yvonne... I'm hoping you tell me you've made progress with our murder cases. Please tell me that. I've had the crime commissioner on the phone again, and he's not a cheerful man."

"You may need to sit down for this one."

"What do you mean?"

"We've found unexpected connections between the two cases."

He scratched his head. "Really? What do you mean?"

She placed several photographs in front of him,

explaining what she had discovered about Wyatt's picture and who was in it.

"So, let me get this straight. Both male victims were in this photo, taken at the time of the Helen Carter and Victoria Mason's disappearance?"

"In a nutshell, yes, we now know the identities of four out of these five men and two of them are dead, recently murdered."

"I see..."

"What I don't yet understand, is why the murdered men never came forward to the original missing person's inquiry. If they knew something, why didn't they present themselves? I don't yet know if Vicky and Helen's murders involved either Guy Davies or Simon Wells, but my suspicion is that someone silenced them after we found the girls' remains."

He ran a hand through his hair. "I admit it sounds like the killer is making sure people can't talk."

"It's possible that some, or all, of the men who circled the girls that day abducted and murdered them. Maybe they kept their secrets all these years, but the discovery of the bones has the conspirators turning on each other."

"What's your next move? I think you should question those men again and find out who the last unknown is."

"I agree, sir. We've got the photographer coming in with his solicitor this afternoon. I thought I'd start with him, then question Adrian Jones and Sam Evans again. I have a feeling they know who the last man is. One or all of them is hiding something. We need answers. I thought you might like to observe the interviews, sir."

"I would, and perhaps we could ask Tasha to review the tapes afterwards. What do you think?"

"Good idea."

"If the killers are targeting witnesses or con-conspirators, we are nowhere near the end of this. It's a mess, but that's excellent work, Yvonne. I've got every faith you will sort this out."

"I've got a great team, sir, we'll get there."

15

VICTIMS OR KILLERS?

Beads of sweat formed on Andrew Wyatt's forehead and upper lip. His left hand clasped his right as though to stop it shaking, and his tie was awry. Damp patches spread through his armpits.

"Can you state your full name for the recording, we have a camera in the corner, and there are observers watching the feed in the room next door," Yvonne began, flanked by Dewi.

Wyatt's solicitor, Mrs Tomlinson, peered at the officers over her glasses. The DI suspected she would keep herself and Dewi on their toes.

"Andrew Alan Wyatt." He sighed seemingly to calm himself.

"And I am Sandra Anne Tomlinson, Andrew's solicitor."

"Thank you, Mrs Tomlinson. I am DI Yvonne Giles, and this is DS Dewi Hughes."

Wyatt cleared his throat. "Can I have a drink of water?"

"Of course." The DI rose from her seat, requesting water from the uniformed officer standing outside.

"Andrew," she began, retaking her seat. "Do you recognise this photograph?" She turned over the first of several pictures on the table.

He frowned, sipping the water. "Of course I do, it's the picture I took of Helen and Victoria dancing at the AberFest music festival in June of two-thousand."

"Tell me who you see in the picture."

He examined the image. "I see... Helen and Victoria, Adrian Jones, and Sam Evans." He sat back in his chair, the movement exaggerated, as though to emphasise that what he had said was all he knew.

"What about the others?" She leaned in. "Who are the three other males in this picture? The ones who are part of the circle around the girls?"

"I told you before, I don't know." He folded his arms.

"Are you afraid of them? Some of them? All of them?"

"What do you mean?"

"Is there a reason you won't identify them to me? Are you afraid?"

"Why would I be afraid?" He fixed her with his stare, but was biting his lower lip.

"My client would appreciate you being specific with your questions." Tomlinson warned.

"Very well, specifically, is there anyone in this photo that you recognise, but are afraid to identify for fear of retribution?"

He shook his head. "No."

"Andrew, two of the men captured in this image are dead. Murdered."

His eyes widened. He swallowed hard.

"It's been all over the news. They pushed one off of Constitution Hill, and the other off the Dam wall at Rhayader."

His mouth hung open. "I watched the news stories."

"I put it to you, that you knew who they were."

"I think you should re-phrase that." Tomlinson suggested.

"Andrew, did you know that this gentleman, she tapped the photograph, was Simon Wells, and this one... was Guy Davies? Both are deceased. Murdered."

He rubbed his chin with one hand, while pulling at his earlobe with the other. The damp patches in his shirt continued to grow. "I didn't know."

"Really? We didn't know who they were either until now. And they never identified themselves in to the initial inquiry. We're trying to figure out why?"

He shrugged. "What has that got to do with me?"

"Why did you take this picture?"

"I told you, the ladies were getting wild, and I thought it would make an interesting photograph. I wanted to capture the atmosphere."

"Yes, but why this image? Why not simply a close-up of the girls?"

"What do you mean?" He frowned.

"It's as though you wanted to photograph the men surrounding them. You wanted to capture all of them."

"I'm sorry, what is your point?" Tomlinson glared at her. "Do you have something on my client? If so, tell us what it is."

"Of course I did." He sighed. "I couldn't capture the atmosphere without getting all of that group in. I wanted the vibe of what was taking place."

"What was taking place?" This time, Dewi asked the question.

Wyatt shrugged, placing his hands in his trouser pockets and stretching his legs. "Two women were dancing, getting loud, and a bunch of young men stood watching."

"Did they know each other? Were they together?" Yvonne asked.

"I don't know."

"You observed them. You photographed them. Did they appear to be together?"

"I think one or two of them spoke to each other? I don't know what they said."

"Did you speak to any of them?"

"I might have done."

"Might have?"

"Okay, I probably did."

"What did you say to them?"

"I can't remember."

"Try."

"Well, I guess it was something like, 'wow, I think they might have had a few too many,' referring to the number of drinks they'd had."

"Was that while the girls were still dancing?"

"No, it was after they had left for the toilets. I think the others were as taken aback as I was at how quickly the ladies' behaviour had gone downhill."

"Meaning?"

"Well, how quickly they had gotten drunk."

"Did any of those men follow the girls?"

"I don't know."

"Did you follow them?"

"No."

"Did you introduce yourself to the others?"

"I think I may have shaken hands with some of them."

"And exchanged names?"

"Maybe."

"Why didn't you tell us this before?"

"You didn't ask me."

"We asked you if you knew the men in the photograph, and if you had met them. You told us you didn't, and you hadn't."

"Well, given that the girls disappeared, the other stuff didn't seem that important. I mean, the girls' vanishing overshadowed everything else. I met many people that weekend, and you couldn't reasonably expect me to remember all of them, I'm not very good at remembering names, I'm afraid."

"Do you admit that the men may have told you who they were when you shook hands?"

He shrugged. "They might have... It was a very long time ago."

"Do you know what I am wondering, Mr Wyatt?"

"What?" He continued to pull at his earlobe.

"I'm wondering why you have been so evasive."

"I haven't been evasive."

"You failed to tell us, when asked, that you had spoken to Adrian Jones during the initial inquiry, and that you had spoken with some, or all, of the other men in your photograph. You told me you had never spoken with any of them."

"I'd forgotten."

"You pursued the conversation with Jones in the police station carpark, even though it must have been clear that he was feeling uncomfortable."

"He should have told me he didn't want to talk. If he didn't say, how would I know? Some people are not very good at making their feelings clear."

"Did you follow the girls to the toilets? You, and perhaps some of the other men?"

"No."

"Did you act as a unit, to pursue those women?"

"No."

"Was your camera work a prelude to something more sinister?"

"No." He placed his head in his hands.

"My client has had enough." Tomlinson put the top on her pen. "Unless you have evidence of any crime, I suggest you end this interview immediately."

The DI nodded, her eyes on Andrew. "You're free to go, but don't leave the country."

~

"He's hiding something." Dewi placed his hands on his hips after Tomlinson and her client had left.

"I agree, Dewi. The problem is, until we figure out what, we are going to get nowhere with him."

"We've had the forensics back on the duct tape used on Wells and Davies."

"Did we get hairs?"

"We got hairs, but only from the victims themselves. However, we also got fibres which were from black dyed wool, possibly belonging to the perpetrator as the victims had no such clothing on them. We don't have the perp's hair."

"What about DNA?"

Dewi shook his head. "I'm afraid we only have DNA of the victims. Whoever killed those men is careful and forensically aware."

"Hmm... What about the white transit? Are we any further with that?"

"We had a plate on CCTV taken around the time they killed Guy Davies. The Reg was an 09. We can't be sure if it is the correct transit, but the timing would fit. It was travelling the coast road. We think it left Aberystwyth via the road to Llangurig."

"That's great, Dewi."

"It would have been..."

"What do you mean?"

"The reg doesn't exist."

"False plates?"

"Looks like it, ma'am."

"Well, at least we have the false plate number, now. So if they use it again, we can track them?"

"It's something to go on, yes."

"I bet they're keeping it in a lockup somewhere."

"I think they probably are." He put his hands in his pockets. "Are we getting Adrian Jones and Sam Evans back in for questioning?"

"Yes, as soon as we can. They are suspects, and they may also be in danger. And that's the problem, we don't really know who the bad guys are. Our suspects could be future victims." She sighed. "We have to consider them all at risk."

"It's messed up." Dewi grimaced.

"You can say that again."

∽

Adrian Jones looked like he'd eaten something which hadn't agreed with him.

He was pale and holding his stomach. The DI worried he might vomit on her shoes.

"Are you all right?" She asked, offering him a seat in the interview room. "We can postpone this, if you'd rather?"

He shook his head. "I want to get it out of the way."

"Very well, if you're sure." She scanned his face. "Are you ill?"

"I had a sleepless night. I'm just tired." His tone was dismissive, but she saw anxiety in his wide eyes.

"I'm sorry you've had to take time off work."

He sighed, folding his arms. "I honestly thought we covered everything last time. What else I can tell you? I have nothing more to say."

"Is anything worrying you?" She tilted her head.

"What do you mean?"

"Are you afraid of anyone?"

"I told you, I'm tired."

"Very well." She retrieved Wyatt's photograph from her paperwork and lay it in front of him.

His eyes moved first to the picture, then to her face, flicking back and fore, trying to work her out. "Why are you showing me this again?"

"It's reminding you we are here because two young women met with a violent death, and you were one of the last people to see them alive. DS Hughes and myself need your help."

"You're beating a dead horse. I told you, I know nothing."

"Look at the other men in the photo."

He shrugged. "What of them?"

"Two of those men are dead." She kept her gaze steady.

"What?" He looked up, his eyes huge in his face. "How?"

"We identified two of the men who were with you, and they both died violent deaths in the last couple of months. They were murdered, Adrian."

He leaned back, running a hand through his hair. "When?"

"You didn't know?" She leaned in. "Haven't you seen the news?"

"No."

She pursed her lips, preparing to deliver the kicker and

watch for his reaction. "Someone killed them after we found the remains of Helen and Victoria. Their names were Guy Davies and Simon Wells. We think they died because of something they knew or something they saw. We think they were murdered so they couldn't tell us what happened."

He gasped. "Did they really know something?"

"We can't say for sure, but it seems likely. At least, the killer thought so."

He ran both hands through his hair, sweat streaming down his temples. "I saw something about those men on TV. I hadn't made the connection, because I didn't recognise them."

"Do their names mean anything to you? Did you know them? Perhaps, you knew them as something else?"

He shook his head. "No, I didn't know them."

"Do you know anything about their murders?"

He swallowed hard. "No, of course I don't. Do you think they might come for me?"

She could see his mind racing, trying to process what he was hearing. "I don't know, Adrian. I suppose that depends on what you saw on the day the girls vanished. You might as well tell us what you know, so we can put the killers away. Stop them hurting anyone else."

He chewed the skin on his knuckle of his right thumb. "I know nothing. The last I saw of the girls, they were heading through the crowd. As for the other men? I barely noticed them. I was having a good time surrounded by others doing the same."

"You said you arrived at the festival in your uncle's car."

"That's right, his Escort."

"Did you use it for anything else?"

"Like what?"

"Like giving anyone a lift? Or for transporting stuff?"

"I had my camping gear in it, nothing else. I didn't give anyone a lift, and I didn't transport any bodies, if that's what you're thinking."

"I'm sorry, Adrian, I wouldn't be doing my job properly if I didn't ask you the important questions, no matter how difficult they may be."

"Am I in danger?" He met her gaze with his own. "Do you think the girls' killer will come after me because of what they think I saw?"

"I don't know... Do you have somewhere you can stay for a while?"

He sipped from the water bottle next to him. "I could ask my parents if I can stay for a few weeks. They'll wonder why."

"Don't tell anyone where you are staying, aside from us. Not your friends, or your work colleagues. I can't tell you if you are in danger, but I think we should assume you are, until we know otherwise. Telephone me and let me know the address you are staying at."

"How long will it take for you to catch these killers?" He took a handkerchief from his trouser pocket and mopped the sweat from his brow.

"We're doing everything we can to get them off the streets. In the meantime, stay with your parents." She passed him her card. "Call me if you need me or if you think of anything else. Call nine, nine, nine, if you think you are in immediate danger. All right?"

"Yes, thank you," he answered, eyes wide.

"We'll do what we can to keep you safe. Let me know as soon as you have a confirmed address."

∼

Sam Evans waited in the interview room, rubbing the scar above his left eye.

His white shirt had crisp creases, and the room smelled of aftershave.

Yvonne was about to interview him on her own, as the rest of her team were busy chasing up leads. Any problems, and she need only call for the uniformed officer outside, but few interviewees acted up once they knew they had a camera on them. She felt safe enough.

"Thank you for coming in, Sam," she began. "I am hoping this won't take too long."

He shrugged. "I've taken the afternoon off."

"Good." She placed papers to her left, and Wyatt's photograph face-down on the table between them.

"I honestly don't know what I can add to the information I gave you last time." He sighed.

"Did you give me information?" She raised her brows.

"Well, you know what I mean. I told you I don't know what happened to the women at the festival. I assume that's why you've called me here again?" He leaned back in his chair, placing both hands in his trouser pockets.

Yvonne turned the photograph over, pushing it towards him.

"You showed me that picture before, and I told you... I was there. I watched them. That's all."

"Tell me about the other men who were there. The ones in this photograph."

"What about them?"

"Did you know any of them?"

"No."

"Did you talk to each other that day, perhaps after this picture was taken? Please look at it."

He frowned. "I don't think so."

"You don't think? Try to recall."

"No, we didn't."

"Really? Not even to discuss the girls' crazy dancing?"

He sighed. "You are obviously looking for something, what is it?"

"Another witness said you all talked together about the girls after they left to go to the toilets. He told me you exchanged names, and handshakes, and banter. Does that ring any bells?"

"You know, honestly? I don't remember."

She pushed the photograph closer to him, pointing to Guy and Simon. "Those two men are dead."

His mouth dropped open, head jerking back.

"Someone killed them within a couple of weeks of each other. Simon Wells died last Friday at Rhayader Dam."

"Bloody hell, I saw that on the news, it was shocking. What happened?"

"We think they abducted him from outside his house." She scrutinised his face. "They pushed guy Davies off the cliffs at Aberystwyth, two weeks before that. The killers bound and gagged both men. That was not a coincidence. I think these men died because we found the remains of Helen Carter and Victoria Mason. Someone in that photograph became worried that the other men would talk. The victims must have known something that put the killer or killers at risk of being caught. What do you think?"

He shook his head, his brow furrowed. "I don't know..."

"I want you to take yourself back to that day at the festival. What did you see? What did you hear? Information you have may be vital."

"I may have spoken with the others, but I don't have a head for names when I am not trying to remember them. I mean, we were out there having fun. These were people I had only just met. I'd been drinking, and I wasn't taking anything too seriously."

"Did you recognise the names, when you heard that Guy and Simon had died?"

"No, the names didn't ring any bells."

"Where were you last Friday evening?"

"I was home."

"Can anyone verify that?"

"My wife saw me, before she left for her shift. She's a nurse in the hospital at Bronglais."

"What time did she leave for her shift?"

"Just after six."

The DI pursed her lips. "That would still give you ample time to get to Rhayader."

"But, I didn't."

"Are you in touch with any of the other men in this picture?"

"No."

"Are you sure?"

"Of course, I'm sure."

"You know we'll be checking your alibi."

"Check it all you want." He glowered at her. "I had nothing to do with the deaths of either Helen and Vicky or Guy and Simon. I can't help you with information, but that doesn't make me a killer."

16

IDENTITY OF THE UNKNOWN MAN

Yvonne believed Wyatt had told the truth when he said that he and the other men had chatted after Helen and Victoria headed for the toilets.

What she needed now was the identity of the last man in the photograph. Perhaps he would be the one with the answers, the pivotal piece in an increasingly complex jigsaw.

She would keep the pressure on Wyatt. If anyone knew the name of the last person in that photo, it was him.

∽

He stood red-faced, hands clenched, and huffing every few seconds.

Yvonne decided it wouldn't do him any harm to wait. Let him ponder the likely reasons for them calling him back in.

When she and Dewi finally took Wyatt into the interview room, he let her have it. "What the hell could you possibly want to know this time? What I had for breakfast? My inside leg measurement? My favourite colour?" His balled fists rested on his hips as he glared at them.

"Please take a seat, Andrew."

"I will not take a seat."

In that moment, she could feel his pent-up anger like a blow to the stomach.

She was glad Dewi was with her, and that they were in an interview room and not a dark alley somewhere. "We'll try not to keep you too long, but that will depend on you." She took her seat at the desk.

"What do you mean?" Wyatt pulled his chair back, slamming it down about a foot away from the table, as though to put distance between himself and the detectives.

She continued. "Andrew, you admitted to us you conversed with the other men in your photograph, and that you had exchanged names."

He frowned. "What of it? It was a long time ago. Why is it even significant? We can't keep going round this. It's getting you nowhere."

"Were they your alibi?"

"What?"

"Who is this man?"

She tapped the face of the remaining unknown individual in the image.

He stared at the picture, then raised his eyes to hers, his chin jutting defiantly. "I don't know."

"I think you do." Her gaze was just as determined as his. "I believe you've known from the beginning."

"This is crazy." He folded his arms. "Anyway, what if I did? So what if I knew that man's name? You can't expect me to remember it now, twenty years later?"

She sighed. "Someone is killing the men in your photo. Perhaps that someone is the man whose identity we don't have." She paused for effect. "He could come for you."

He frowned. "Why? I am not even in the picture."

"But you took it, didn't you? And anybody who has looked at old newspaper clippings, or watched old news stories, or read up on the internet, would have heard of you and your photograph, wouldn't they?"

"I guess..."

"What if you are also on their hit list? What if the killer is this unknown male, and he thinks you witnessed something that day? Even now he might be planning your death. Why wouldn't you want to help us by giving us his name? Or, is it because it doesn't worry you? Is it because you murdered the girls? Is it because you are the one who is eliminating potential witnesses?"

"All right, all right." He held his hands up. "I think I remember his name."

"Thank you." She leaned in. "Who is he?"

"His name is Paul. I think it's Paul Hughes."

"Do you know where he is now?"

"No." Wyatt shook his head.

She turned to Dewi. "Can you speak to the DCI about a national appeal?"

He nodded. "I'll get on it."

The DI returned her attention to Wyatt. "Why didn't you tell us this earlier? It could have saved Simon Wells' life."

Wyatt chewed the inside of his cheek, brushing his trousers with his hands.

She pushed her card towards him. "If you have any other details, you think we should know, make sure you call me. Lives could depend on it, including yours. You don't do yourself any favours by withholding information."

～

AJ HAD FINISHED his shift at the supermarket.

They watched him as he made his way around the side of the building where staff parked their cars. It was quarter past eight and dark, save for the sparse street lamps and the light emanating from the store.

They couldn't kidnap him there. They would be all over the CCTV footage on the cameras dotted around. But they could follow him to somewhere more convenient.

It wouldn't matter if the cameras captured the transit. White vans were common as muck, and they had four false plates on rotation. But they couldn't risk themselves on camera, not with the technology available these days. It wouldn't matter about the balaclavas, the latest cameras could identify them by their gait.

They sat in silence until the driver tapped his thumbs on the steering wheel.

"Come on... Come on..." He forced the words through gritted teeth. "For Christ's sake, get on with it."

"What's he doing?" his passenger asked, wiping away the condensation on his side of the windscreen.

"He's moving something around in the boot, looks like he's taking shopping back with him, and he hasn't got the space for it."

Finally, Adrian Jones climbed into the driver's seat and fired up his engine.

The transit's passenger put on his balaclava, tossing another into the lap of the driver, as the van followed the Corsa into the dark lanes heading out of town.

Jones had recently moved into his parents' detached home in the hamlet of Aberbechan, leading his would-be killers to change their plans at short notice. This had darkened their mood considerably, even though there were fewer houses in Aberbechan, meaning less chance of being seen, and no CCTV.

AJ always parked in the lay-by just before his parents' house. It was as good a spot as any to capture him, but they would have to be sharp. He would be outside for only a minute. They needed to follow close enough to be there in time, but not so near as to make him suspicious. He may already be nervous if he remembered who Guy Davies and Simon Wells were, and they believed he did. Given the enormity of the events that took place at the AberFest that fateful summer, they felt sure he would not have forgotten. None of them would. He would be looking over his shoulder. They couldn't afford to mess this up.

They slowed right down on the approach to Aberbechan. AJ's Corsa approached the lay-by.

Somewhere in the darkness an owl hooted.

AJ looked up at the half-moon, before walking round to the boot to retrieve his shopping.

The transit occupants jumped out, leaving the engine running and the doors open.

Their victim dropped his shopping as they pulled the hood over his head, forcing him up against the car to zip-tie his hands behind his back. They pulled the bag tight around his neck with a drawstring, muffling his cries. After binding his ankles, they bundled him into the back of the van.

Leaving on their leather gloves, they removed their balaclavas and drove away, home free.

17

KIDNAPPED

Paul Hughes walked into Newtown police station two days after they launched a national appeal with his name and photograph.

Now living in Llandovery, he had driven an hour and a half to be interviewed by detectives.

Hughes was the manager of a dairy farm, and entered the station at eleven-thirty in the morning, having set off after completing his morning workload.

Though Yvonne had never met Hughes, he was high on her suspect list.

She was preparing for a manhunt, when in he walked, wearing mud-stained overalls with the sleeves rolled up to the elbows. His neatly combed, mid-length hair seemed at odds with the rest of his creased and weathered appearance.

"I heard you wanted to see me," he said as she collected him from reception. "I saw it in the news, that you were looking for me, like. You could have phoned me like normal person. I nearly had a heart attack."

He had a warm Welsh lilt to his voice and appeared genuinely bewildered at all the attention.

"I'm sorry, Mister Hughes," she began. "We wanted to talk to you, and we didn't know where you were. We only had your name and an old photograph. The national appeal seemed our only option."

"It was my wife who saw it on the telly. She told me you wanted me for questioning. Well, I've done nothing wrong, I said, so she said I should come in and find out what it's all about, like."

Yvonne nodded. "Well, thank you, Mister Hughes."

"It's Paul. You can call me Paul."

"Paul, I'm hoping you can help us with an investigation into the abduction and murder of two young women in the summer of two-thousand. We found their remains a few weeks ago, in Warren Wood. Did you hear about that? It has been in the news a lot."

"I heard that they'd been found, yes. It was awful, what happened to those girls. No-one deserves that, like."

"Quite... So, you work on a farm?"

"I've been on farms since I was a boy. Grew up on 'em. I run one now, like. You can't beat the outdoors. You wouldn't get me behind a desk somewhere. Anyway, with all this muck on my hands, I'd make a mess of all the paperwork." He grinned at her, but the DI noticed he spoke as though his mouth was dry.

He wiped his palms on his thighs, his brows raised as he waited for her to say something.

She thought he looked like a bewildered child. Her instinct was to put him at ease, and yet the man in front of her might be a cold-blooded killer.

The DI kept her mothering instinct in check. "Do you

remember being at AberFest music festival, the year Helen Carter and Victoria Mason vanished?"

He nodded. "I remember being there, and them going missing. It was all over the papers and the telly."

"Did you watch the news bulletins?" She tilted her head, watching for his reaction.

"I saw one or two."

"What did you think?"

"Well, like everyone else, I thought it was strange how they disappeared. I felt sorry for the families, like."

"What did you think happened to them?"

"Back then, I thought they'd probably gone off on their own for a while, like. You know, backpacking and whatnot."

"You didn't suspect foul-play?"

"I probably did, but I didn't think it likely. Some people choose to disappear, don't they?"

"They do, but those girls had no reason to wander off. As the news coverage stated, they were about to go to college. It would have been out of character to run away when they had worked so hard to achieve their university places, don't you think?"

He shrugged. "Well, you found their bodies, so now I know someone murdered them."

She pushed Wyatt's photograph towards him. "Do you remember this picture being taken?"

"I don't remember it being taken, but I know I was at that festival, and I remember those girls."

"Your wife recognised you in this image."

"Yes, she spotted me, but only after you enhanced it and highlighted me. It made me stand out, like. She didn't spot me in the original."

"Would you have recognised yourself?"

"I daresay, I would've done, yes."

"But, you didn't..."

"Well, I wasn't watching the TV, my wife was. I was mucking out the yard when she called me in and told me I was on telly, like."

"You said you remembered the girls."

"That's right, yeah."

"And you heard about their disappearance at the time they vanished."

"Yeah."

"Then, you must have seen the appeals for information at the time?"

"I didn't think I had anything to add to what people had told police already. I thought they had enough witnesses."

"Did you know police were looking for you?"

"No." He shook his head.

"They wanted to talk to all those who had seen the girls that day, and most especially the people in this photograph. And, in the picture, you are staring at Helen and Victoria."

"I wasn't staring."

"There was something different about these girls, and the way they were dancing, wasn't there?" She kept her gaze on him. "Did you notice that? You saw them, what were you thinking?"

He shrugged. "They were nice-looking girls, and they were having a good time. They were putting on a show, like."

"Putting on a show? What do you mean by that?"

"Well, you know, getting carried away. They were throwing themselves about, like."

"Did you see them drinking?"

"Er, they were drinking beers, I think? I didn't see them drinking much, if I recall rightly. I saw them maybe take a few sips. They must have drunk a lot more than that, though."

"What makes you say that?"

"Well, they were falling over... banging into people. We were giving them a wide berth, like."

"Were you worried about them?"

"No, I just thought they were having a laugh. I didn't see any reason to be worried. People get drunk all the time, they don't usually disappear."

"Tell me about the other men in this picture."

"What about them?"

"Do you remember them?"

"Not really..."

She pushed the image closer to him. "Have a good look at it."

He picked it up.

"Is that jogging your memory?"

"I remember seeing one or two of them."

"Do you remember talking to them?"

"I may have."

"What did you talk about?"

"I think it was a bit of banter about the music and the beer."

"What about the girls? Did you discuss them with the others?"

"I don't know, maybe, probably did."

"Several of the other men stated you were discussing the ladies, after they had stopped dancing and headed for the toilets."

He shrugged. "Maybe I did then."

"Are you telling me you don't actually remember doing that?"

"I think I discussed them being out of it, so to speak."

"Did you follow the girls, after they left to go to the toilet? Perhaps, with some of the other men?"

"No."

"Are you sure about that? Maybe you intended helping them get to the toilets because of how intoxicated they were?"

"I didn't follow them."

"Did anyone else follow them? Look at the photograph again and let me know if you witnessed any of those men going after the girls."

He stared at the image, turning it about in his hands. "No, I didn't see any of these men going after them."

"What about the man who took this photo? Do you remember him?"

Hughes ran a hand through his hair. "Oh God, it was so long ago."

"Think about it, take your time. If you don't remember, then you don't, but take a moment to picture him. He had a brand new digital SLR camera. He may have come up to you to show you the picture on the screen."

"Wait..." He rubbed his cheek. "I do remember him. He did come over to talk to me and the others."

"What did he say?"

"He was trying too hard."

"In what way?"

"Well, the music and everything was pretty loud, and he was shouting in my ear at one point. I think he did that with the others, too, like he was desperate to talk to someone. I really didn't feel like talking to him, but I could see he wanted to be friendly, so I tried."

"Do you remember if he introduced himself?"

"He did, yeah."

"Can you remember his name?"

"No."

"Do you know his name now?"

He shook his head. "No, he told me, but I can't remember what he said. It was so long ago."

"Does the name Andrew Wyatt mean anything to you?"

"Yes!" Hughes' eyes lit up. "He called himself Andy. He was thinking of becoming a journalist, I think. Andy, yes that's it." He appeared relieved at regaining the memory. "I got there in the end. Wait..." He frowned.

"What? Have you remembered something else?"

"He followed the girls."

"Did he?"

"Yes, he chatted with us, and then he stood behind, watching the band. I felt relieved he wasn't shouting in my ear anymore, and I looked around for him to make sure I was safe, but he had gone from his spot. As I looked about, I saw him disappearing into the crowd in the direction the girls had gone."

"Really?" She made a note.

"Yes."

"How much time had passed between the girls leaving, and Andy disappearing in their direction, would you say?"

"Only about ten minutes..."

"Are you sure, Paul?"

"Yes, only a couple of songs had gone by. I knew this, because I worried he might return and start shouting in my ear again."

"I see."

"Can I go now?"

"Paul, have you seen any of the men in this photo, since that day? Have any of them approached you? Are you in touch with any of them?"

He shook his head. "No."

"You're sure about that?"

"Yes."

"Would you be willing to make a statement, including everything you've told me about Andy's behaviour that day?"

"Sure," he affirmed.

"Thank you, and yes, you can go. I may need to speak with you again, however."

"Well, you know where I am. I'm up at Henllys Dairy Farm, near Llandovery. I'm always there. My wife tells me I'm never home."

"We'll need your home address, too, and any phone numbers you have."

"No problem."

The DI pondered his information. Andrew Wyatt had not disclosed following the girls. In fact, he had explicitly denied doing so. The question was, why? It put him firmly in the frame. Perhaps, by making himself such a nuisance to some of the other people there, he had hoped to give himself an alibi. Either way, he had some explaining to do.

∽

Yvonne's phone buzzed on the dresser.

She woke with a start. "Yvonne Giles."

"Sorry, ma'am-"

"Callum?" She glanced at the clock. It was two in the morning. "What is it?"

"One of our suspects has disappeared."

"What? Who?" She rubbed her eyes, swinging her legs out of bed.

"Adrian Jones. We think someone took him from outside his parents' home. He left his car in the lay-by. The boot was wide open and there was shopping in it, some of which had spilled into the road. His parents haven't seen him. They were expecting him back by eight-thirty last night, but he didn't arrive at the house. SOCO are on their way to examine the vehicle now, ma'am."

"Can you do me a favour, Callum?"

"Of course."

"Can you phone the DCI and ask him to request a warrant to search the home and business premises of Andrew Wyatt, on suspicion of the murder of Helen Carter and Victoria Mason. I think Wyatt may have Adrian Jones. We'll need that warrant ASAP. Where are you now?"

"I'm at the station, ma'am."

"Good, I'll meet you there. We can't do much at AJ's parents' place, but we can prep to raid Wyatt's property. Uniformed officers can accompany us, and we'll need a tactical arms team on standby. Probably a canine unit, too. If Jones is there, the dogs should find him."

"What shall I tell the DCI, ma'am?"

"Sorry?" She frowned.

"Your reasons for suspecting Wyatt?"

"Oh, I see. Paul Hughes made a statement alleging that Wyatt followed Helen Carter and Victoria Mason on the day they went missing. Something he has always denied. The statement may be tenuous, but it's all we've got and, if Wyatt has Jones, the clock is ticking. We have to move. Wyatt is the only one who knew the names of the other men watching the girls that day. I think he has to be mixed up in their murders somehow. Please ask the DCI to pull out all the stops. Tell him Jones' life may depend on it."

"Right, ma'am. I'll get on it."

"Are you all right, Yvonne? What's going on?" Tasha sat up, blinking in the light of the bedside lamp.

"I have to go out, Tasha. I think someone has kidnapped

one of my witnesses. The abductors will murder him, I've got to go,"

"Right." Her partner jumped out of bed. "You get dressed, I'll make you a coffee. You'll need your wits about you."

"Thank you." Yvonne headed for the bathroom.

"And please, be safe out there... I know what you're like when you get the bit between your teeth."

The DI poked her head around the door, toothbrush in hand. "I'll be careful, I promise. Besides, there will be a heavy police presence. We don't know how many kidnappers we are dealing with. We'll be taking no chances."

"I've been working on profiles." Tasha called from the kitchen. "I can tell you about it tomorrow."

18

THE RED BACKPACK

Wyatt's red-brick, five bedroom detached home lay within a thousand yards of the outdoor centre he co-owned with his wife, Yvette.

As well as the centre itself, there were several outbuildings, and a hundred and fifty acres of land comprising woodland, grassland, and mountainous terrain. An ideal place to make a person disappear, Yvonne thought. If Wyatt had Jones, they had to find them fast.

She felt nauseous on the drive to the station to meet Callum. Deep breaths helped, but didn't entirely take the feeling away.

After parking her car, she took a deep glug of the coffee-to-go prepared by Tasha, and ran to the station doors.

"How far have we got with the warrant?" she asked Callum as he sorted their tactical gear.

"The DCI was arranging it from his home. He said he'd ring me as soon as they agreed it and we should get something from the judge via email."

"Great."

"Dewi and Dai are on their way in, ma'am."

She smiled. "This team is a credit to the service. What would I do without you?"

"We'd better armour up, ma'am." He grinned. "We do our best."

∽

A TACTICAL ARMS UNIT, in full body armour and headgear, filed out of the transit, moving silently into position until they had the home of Andrew Wyatt surrounded.

The dogs remained in the smaller canine van, their handlers on standby.

Yvonne had the warrant in the front pocket of her stab vest. It covered all of Wyatt's premises, but the DI thought it best to start with the house and outbuildings. If he had taken AJ, he would be unlikely to keep him in the business centre. She was sure he would consider that too risky.

The tactical unit's commanding officer approached her as she stood at the sturdy, double gates to the property. "We're ready to go when you are." He lifted his protective glasses so that she could see his eyes. A mask and helmet covered the rest of his face. "We'll do the sweep while you guys search."

She nodded. "Thank you, can you have someone watch the business centre, just in case he makes a run for it over there?"

"We're monitoring all the buildings." He nodded. "You've got the warrant?"

She tapped her stab vest. "Safe and sound."

"Give us the nod when you're ready," he said, before returning to his unit.

Motion-sensor light flooded the yard. Beyond this, the night was black.

Two armoured officers stood at the entrance to Wyatt's home with an enforcer, ready to bash open the doors for the swift entry.

The DI, Dewi, and Callum assumed position ready to follow them in. Dai brought up the rear.

She gave the nod.

"Armed police! Open up!" the forward tactical officer called.

"Armed police, open up!" he repeated.

Receiving no response, they smashed the door open, shattering two of the small panes in the windowed arch above.

Lights came on in the house. A man shouted and a woman screamed.

"Police! Come down with your hands on your head!"

Andrew Wyatt appeared at the top of the stairs in a pair of black boxers, blinking in the torchlight.

They allowed him time to put on a t-shirt and jeans, before cuffing and leaving him with Yvonne, who led him into the kitchen, holding up the papers. "Mister Wyatt, we have a warrant to search your properties."

"Why?" He frowned, holding his hand up to protect his eyes from the light. He looked back towards the stairs, where his wife stood, fully clothed, flanked by a female officer.

Yvette Wyatt appeared angry and frightened, her hands balled into fists. "What's going on?" she asked as they escorted her to the lounge.

The tactical unit continued their sweep through the house, while the DI's team began a systematic search of each room, looking for Adrian Jones and evidence of his kidnap.

Yvonne stayed with Wyatt. "Mister Wyatt, we have a warrant to search your home and property in connection with the disappearance of Adrian Jones."

"What? I haven't seen Adrian Jones. What the hell are you talking about?"

"I am also arresting you on suspicion of the abduction and murder of Helen Carter and Victoria Mason. You do not have to say anything..."

As she continued to caution him, he opened and shut his mouth several times but did not resist.

Callum rejoined her. "We're bagging all dark clothing. There are a couple of jumpers which could be a match for the fibres found on Guy Davies."

She nodded. "Good."

Wyatt strained at the cuffs behind his back. "What are you taking about? I didn't murder Guy Davies."

The DI noted he hadn't denied killing Helen and Vicky. She led him to a waiting van, placing him in the caged area at the back.

Meanwhile, the search of the premises continued.

Dewi joined her near the gates.

"Find anything?"

He shook his head. "Nothing so far, but his wife has given us the keys to the centre, and we have the outbuildings to go through after the house."

"All right, Dewi. I don't think we'll find Jones in the centre. The outbuildings are the most likely hiding place."

"The dogs are in there, I think they'd be barking by now if they'd got a scent."

Yvonne scratched her head. "Damn, I felt sure he'd be here."

"Well, he might be... We'll keep looking."

"Can you stay with the search, Dewi? I'm going to take Callum and go with the prisoner back to the station. We'll get him booked in and begin questioning. I know I can trust you to make sure the search here is thorough."

"You can, ma'am."

Her head hurt. She wondered whether she had got this all wrong. As they made the journey back to custody, she pondered the possibility that someone else abducted AJ and the others. Perhaps Wyatt had paid someone. Maybe he was in cahoots with another, such as Sam Evans.

Her gut told her Wyatt had a role in Helen and Vicky's murder. Proving it, however, was another matter.

∽

Wyatt sat stony-faced, his arms folded.

Yvonne sat opposite, flanked by Callum. "Tell me about the girls."

Callum gave the suspect a copy of his festival photograph showing the young women. To the side of this, he placed other images of the Helen and Vicky taken by friends and family.

"There's nothing to tell." He spat the words, refusing to look at the photos.

"We know you followed them."

He kept his eyes on the table.

"Right after you took that photo of them dancing, you went up to each of those men and introduced yourself."

"No comment."

"You found out their names, didn't you?"

"No comment."

"I put it to you, that your intention was to give yourself an alibi."

"No comment."

"People would assume that it couldn't have been you abducting the girls, because you were busy having a laugh and a joke with the others."

"No comment."

"But, they saw you disappearing into the crowd, ten minutes after the girls had done the same."

"No comment."

"Did you slip something into their drinks? What was it?"

"No comment."

"Had you only planned to rape them?"

"No comment."

"Did something go wrong?"

"No comment."

"Or was the whole thing planned from the start? Abduction, rape, and murder?"

"No comment."

"Did you decide to kill witnesses because we found the girls' remains?"

"No comment."

"Because you could be charged with murder."

"No comment."

"Did they cry, Helen and Victoria? Did they beg you for their lives?"

"Stop! Stop!" Wyatt put his head in his hands. "I want my solicitor."

Yvonne leaned back in her chair. "Very well, interview suspended until Mrs Tomlinson arrives. DC Jones will bring you a cup of tea and something to eat."

Sandra Tomlinson yawned as she requested to see her client alone before the interview continued.

Yvonne checked her watch. It was almost six in the morning.

Dai and Dewi were still at Wyatt's place with the ongoing search. The tactical team had left, leaving uniform, and the dogs to help finish the job.

Callum came to find her as she poured a coffee. "Tomlinson tells me they are ready for us, ma'am."

She envied how fresh he looked. The only clue that he had been hard at it since the small hours was the faint stubble peppering his usually smooth skin.

She gulped some of the hot coffee. "Right, let's get to it."

~

"Tell us what happened after you followed the girls through the crowd?"

"Where is your evidence that my client followed the girls at all? You only have the word of a man who was also watching the girls dance, and who himself ought to be on your suspect list."

"He is."

Tomlinson regarded the DI with a raised brow. "You mean your principal witness is also one of your suspects."

"Yes."

"Well, unless you have evidence to back up your claims, I suggest you de-arrest my client. You have no solid grounds to keep him here."

Wyatt scowled. "Even if I went to the toilets, your witness said I did so ten minutes after the girls. It was a large crowd. How would I have found them?"

The DI levelled her gaze at Wyatt. "You could have easily caught up with them, even if it had been twenty minutes after they left. They were falling all over the place. Abducting them would have been a piece of cake when they were in that state."

He folded his arms.

"Did they cry?"

"DI Giles, I request you stop this interview now, and de-arrest my client, unless you have evidence to put to him to back up your preposterous claims."

Wyatt's mouth had turned down, and he was steadfastly avoiding her gaze.

She was sure she had her man, but Tomlinson would not budge an inch.

Yvonne changed tack. "Perhaps it wasn't you. At least, not on your own. Did you agree with any of the others to have fun with girls? Maybe-"

"Ma'am?" Dewi's head popped around the door. "Sorry to disturb you, but can I have a quick word?"

"Interview suspended six-thirty. We'll reconvene in five minutes."

She joined her sergeant, who had just returned from Wyatt's property. "What is it? Have you found Jones?"

"No, ma'am, but we found a red nylon backpack belonging to Victoria Mason. It's the one she had with her when she disappeared. We found it under a ton of animal feed."

"Wow... Can we be sure that it's Victoria's? We'll need DNA confirmation, surely."

"It's still got her notebook, camera, and other bits and pieces in there, Yvonne. We can be pretty sure it belonged to her. We took a quick look through the photos, and there are pictures of both Helen and Victoria, and of the festival. There's no doubt in my mind, ma'am."

"Did you find the girls' phones?"

"No, but we already have enough to charge Andrew Wyatt with two counts of murder."

19

A COMPLEX WEB

Adrian Jones' shook so much, his seat rattled on the floor as they ripped the hood off his head.

Harsh lamps stung his eyes, and he was sure these men were about to beat and kill him.

The room was cold and dark aside from the light in his face.

He knew they were there, somewhere in the blackness behind the lights.

They had tied his ankles to the legs of the chair and bound his hands with zip-ties behind his back. Sweat streamed from his body.

They hadn't hit him, yet.

"What do you want?" Though his eyes were wide in terror, his pupils were pinpricks in the glare.

"You don't have to do this." He was about to lose control of his bladder. He had already done so once. "Please? Please tell me what this is about? I know nothing. Really, I don't. If this is about those girls, and what you did to them, I saw nothing. If you did it, if you killed them, I wouldn't know. I can't tell people what I do not know. Please believe me..." He sobbed. "I don't want to die. Hello? Hello?"

Silence followed the sound of a door opening and closing.
Adrian shivered alone in the darkness.

∽

ANDREW JOHN WYATT, you are being charged with the murders of Helen Carter and Victoria Mason. I must remind you, you are still under caution.

"What's this?" Tomlinson glowered. "Where is your evidence? We have a right to know what it is."

There was a knock on the door.

"Come in." The DI kept her eyes on Wyatt as she accepted the evidence bag containing the backpack from Dewi.

The colour drained from the suspect's face.

"Andrew, please note exhibit DH1, a red nylon backpack which we believe belonged to Victoria Mason."

Wyatt stared at the bag, his right hand clenched in his left.

"Do you know where we found it?"

Wyatt and his solicitor were silent.

"We found it in one of your outbuildings, under bags of animal feed. From the look of it, it had been there for a considerable time. Can you tell me how it got there?"

Tomlinson stared at her client, as though hoping for a reasonable excuse.

"What did you do with the girls' phones? Do you still have those? Or did you destroy them? Was it too risky to keep their mobiles as trophies, the way you did with their bag? The phones would have led police to you, wouldn't they?"

Wyatt was silent.

"Did you kill them in that outbuilding, Andrew? Then

bury them back in the Wood, near to where you abducted them? Is that what you did?"

Silence.

"Crime scene investigators are on their way to your premises right now, and a unit with cadaver dogs. You can't hide anymore. If there are traces there, they will find them."

Silence.

"Why don't you tell us what happened? This is a chance to give your side of the story."

The suspect maintained his silence.

"Where is Adrian Jones?" she asked, aware the clock was ticking. If Wyatt was working with someone else, they might panic when they realised he was in custody, and do away with their captive and any evidence.

"Andrew, where is Adrian Jones?" She repeated.

"I don't know."

"Andrew, if you murdered those girls, we will have the evidence of that soon. Let's stop this, shall we? Let's not create any more victims."

He ran both hands through his hair. "Look, I don't know where Adrian Jones is. I know nothing about the other men's murders, either. I can't tell you who killed them, because I do not know."

"And the girls?"

Wyatt's face puffed, becoming bright red.

"Did you kill the girls?"

Silence.

"Andrew?"

He exhaled like a burst balloon. "All right, all right... I killed the girls. I didn't mean to. Everything went wrong. It got out of hand. I thought we could have fun. I took them for a drive. It got out of hand."

"I'd like to speak with my client alone, before we continue." Tomlinson held up her hand. "I'll need about an hour to confer with him."

"Very well." The DI nodded. Then, looking at Wyatt, she tilted her head. "Andrew, did you give those men's names to anyone else? Did you tell anyone who the boys in your photograph were?"

20

SAND IN THE HOURGLASS

Adrian Jones had spent ages trussed up inside the back of the van.

He didn't know how long, but it was enough that every part of him ached.

He had cried, fought his bonds, banged his head on the van floor trying to get someone's attention, and had now resorted to tears again.

Sure he was going to die, he thought of the ones he loved, and prayed for only the second time in his life. He begged to be spared.

The doors in the front opened and slammed. He could hear the men conversing, but the noise of the engine revving up, and the rattling of the van as they moved off, prevented him making out the words.

Each time the van drove over a bump, AJ hit his head. Holding it off the floor ached his neck and was hard to do for more than a few minutes at a time.

Every second increased his dread of what was coming. He tried to follow the journey in his head but, in a mind wracked with terror, it was an impossible task.

∽

"ANDREW..." Yvonne pressed him. "Did you tell anybody the names of the men in your photograph? I want you to think. Try to remember. Adrian Jones' life may depend on it."

"No... Not for a long time."

"What do you mean a long time?"

"Not since... since..."

"Since you killed Helen and Vicky?"

"No, since the search in the days afterwards."

"Who did you tell? It certainly wasn't the police."

"I told Helen's father." Wyatt hung his head.

"You mean Peter Carter?"

"Yes. He came looking for me, after I handed that photo in to the police. Newspapers and television reporters identified me, and he came to see me. Told me I was a dead man unless I gave him the names of the lads who had been watching his daughter. He was so angry. I gave him the names."

"I see. You gave Carter the identities, but you didn't give them to police because, of course, those men were the only ones who could point a finger at you. God... Did Carter say why he wanted the names?"

"I thought he was going to pass the information on to the enquiry... but he didn't. I was terrified I would get a knock on my door, but it never came. Two of the men I photographed presented themselves of their own volition, anyway. I didn't think it would make any difference, giving the names to Carter."

"We'll take full statements from you regarding what happened to the girls... what you did. But, right now, I have a man's life to save. An innocent person you inadvertently put at risk. These officers will take you to custody, where you'll have a list of formal charges to discuss with your solicitor. I have a job to do."

She left him with Tomlinson and the two officers who would escort him to the custody suite.

Within twenty minutes, Yvonne and her team were heading to the homes of Peter Carter and Berwyn Mason.

Yvonne, Dewi, and several armed officers headed to Carter's home, while Dai and Callum went with armed police to Mason's house.

At this stage, they did not know where Adrian Jones was, but Wyatt's information had convinced the DI that Carter must have him. And, if Helen's father wasn't working on his own, his partner in crime might well be Vicky's dad, Mason.

Carter had known the identities of the men in the picture since the beginning, but had sat on that information. He hadn't been sure which of them had abducted and murdered his daughter, or even that his daughter was dead. The finding of the girls' remains had led to him exacting his revenge.

Ironic, Yvonne mused, that the real perpetrator was the one who had supplied the false trail to both the grieving fathers, and police. Wyatt had played them all.

21

FRANTIC SEARCH

Armed officers filed around the back of the Carters' home and flanked The DI and Dewi as they waited on the porch for the door to be answered.

Celia Carter's hand trembled as she opened it, smoothing her light floral dress.

"Mrs Carter?" Yvonne took a step forward.

"I don't want any trouble..." Celia stared wide-eyed at the armed officers.

"Is your husband in?"

The frightened woman shook her head. "He's not here. I don't know where he is, he left early."

"Did he say where he was going?"

"No."

"Did he say when he'd be back?"

"He said he'd be back later."

"Mrs Carter, we have a warrant to search your home. Does your husband have a computer or laptop? And we'll need his mobile phone number."

Celia moved back, allowing them into her home.

With his number, they could attempt to ping his phone,

triangulating its position. His Google searches might provide the location to which he would take his victim. It was a longshot, but worth trying.

"What vehicle was your husband driving?" Yvonne stayed with Celia Carter while the others conducted the search.

"A white van... Ford transit, I think."

"Do you have the registration of the vehicle?"

She shook her head.

"Where does your husband keep his papers?"

"In the spare bedroom."

"Thank you." The DI left Mrs Carter in the company of a female officer while she headed upstairs.

Dewi was with another officer, scrolling through Carter's laptop. Fortuitously, the latter hadn't bothered with password protection. It would save them precious time.

Yvonne combed through reams of paperwork, looking for details of the white transit. She found nothing.

After they gave Carter's mobile number to Newtown station, they pinged his phone to a location near Oswestry.

Dewi had also come up trumps with his Carter's Google searches. He'd been looking up Pistyll Rhaeadr, a waterfall approximately four miles from the village of Llanrhaeadr-ym-Mochnant, in the north of Powys, sixteen miles west of Oswestry.

With both the mobile location and the Google searches coinciding, they knew it was more than coincidence.

Dewi gave Yvonne a knowing look. "It's the tallest waterfall in Wales," he said, his expression grim. "They're going to throw him off the bloody top. It's two hundred and forty feet high."

"Oh, God..." The DI felt a lump form in her throat. "We need a response team at that location as soon as possible."

THEY PARKED the transit in a lay-by, the only free parking for the falls.

The cafe and carpark were to be avoided at all costs. It would probably have CCTV cameras, and they had to get their captive up the falls without attracting attention.

They pushed the bound man in front of them, using a stick to prod him in the back.

If they encountered anyone else up there, they could move in close, hiding his tied hands from view. But they were not expecting company. It was still too early in the season for any but the most hardened of walkers, and they did not intend hanging about to meet any.

They took a right off the lane before reaching the tea rooms, passed through a gate onto a footpath which rose through woodland and areas of stone walling, and through another gate which led to open, mountainous terrain.

The would-be victim struggled with the climb in his black lace-ups which were now soaked through.

Carter and Mason's walking boots had no such issues, and Mason trekked without the limp he had affected for the DI and Dewi.

With a stream to their right, they took a pathway to their left, which led them to the top of the waterfall, still jabbing the shivering AJ to keep him moving.

The views through the valley, even in the mist and drizzle, were something else. On any other day, and especially before their daughters' bones were found, Carter and Mason might have walked this scenic route in the Berwyn Mountains for pleasure. Mason had, after all, been conceived there. But the stone walling, hills, streams, and woods held no attraction for them today. They were focused only on their grim task.

They crossed the stream, and forced their captive over a stile, to join the footpath on the opposite side of the valley. There was still almost a mile to go, to reach the ridge of Moel Sych. The walk was all part of it. They wanted their victim to ponder the role he had played in their daughters' demise.

When they eventually reached the top of Pistyll Rhaeadr, a light drizzle had begun.

It wouldn't be long until AJ suffered the same fate as the others.

22

RACE TO PISTYLL RHEAEDR

The DI rang Tasha on the way to Llanrhaeadr-ym-Mochnant.

"Yvonne? Is everything all right?"

"Don't worry about me, love, I'm absolutely fine."

The psychologist sighed with relief. "Thank God, where are you?"

"We're on our way to the falls at Pistyll Rhaeadr, to what may be a hostage situation. I think the victim is being taken to the top of the waterfall, and they're intending to throw him off. We have to convince Peter Carter and Berwyn Mason that the man they are holding is innocent of the murder of their daughters."

Tasha paused. "Are you going to the top of the falls?"

Yvonne could hear the anxiety in her partner's voice. "We'll be close to it, yes. As close as we can get without making the situation worse for the victim."

"I'm coming," Tasha declared. "I will be with you as soon as I can. You might need me."

The DI considered dissuading her, but the psychologist's

determination was obvious, and she had experience in dealing with difficult hostage situations. They might need her expertise to persuade Carter and Mason of AJ's innocence.

"All right," she agreed. "But you'll stay with me throughout, and no heroics."

"I don't think I'm the one in danger of heroics, DI Giles." Tasha retorted.

"We'll see you there, Tasha. There will be a significant police presence. Just follow the line of parked vehicles."

"Okay, stay safe, Yvonne."

The DI had a call waiting.

It was the DCI. "Yvonne?"

"Yes, sir."

"What's going on? I have a request for armed backup and a police helicopter for Llanrhaeadr."

"It's for the falls, sir. And, yes, we need you to sanction a possible armed intervention for a hostage rescue from the top of the Pistyll Rhaeadr waterfall. I would advise not having the chopper there to begin with. It might be better on standby until we know what we're dealing with. We want nothing up there that would scare them into falling off. But, if they go to ground, we may need it to help locate them. If we mess this up, I believe they will throw our victim from the top of the falls."

"Jesus..."

"Yes, it's a very delicate situation, sir, and we'll need all the help you can arrange."

"Right, leave it with me. And, Yvonne?"

"Sir?"

"Don't put yourself in harm's way."

"Right, sir."

~

APPROACHING the top of Pistyll Rhaeadr, visibility was steadily reducing. Clouds hung low as the drizzle thickened. The temperature had dropped several degrees.

Their captive shook from a mixture of fear and cold. Carter repeatedly pushed him in the back to keep him moving. Several times this resulted in AJ falling over, covering his shirt and trousers with wet mud.

Adrian walked backwards, trying to plead with them through the duct tape over his mouth, eyes doing their best to persuade.

Carter pushed him some more.

Within twenty feet of the top of the falls, AJ ran at his captors, shouldering each in the chest, before running down the slope as fast as the conditions and his shoes would allow.

Stunned, Carter and Mason started after him, the latter cursing under his breath. They were too close for this to go wrong now.

AJ had put several metres between himself and his abductors. Even with his hands behind his back, he had youth on his side, but they were gaining on him.

Desperate, he pushed harder but found it difficult to control the run.

The fall was inevitable. He thudded onto his chest, continuing into a horizontal roll down the slope, with his two kidnappers giving chase.

When they finally caught up with their him, Carter kicked AJ so hard in the stomach that the beleaguered man vomited and lay heaving, trying to catch his breath.

Carter was unrepentant. He reached down and yanked AJ by the arm, forcing him into an upright position.

Mason took the opposite limb, and they half-pushed, half-

dragged their hapless victim back up towards the falls, hanging onto him the whole way.

There was no-one around to see. They were within sight of the top. Their mission was almost complete.

23

STAND-OFF

Yvonne, Dewi, and the armed officers they had travelled with, clambered out of the van after driving it as close as they could to the falls.

They found what they suspected was Carter and Mason's white transit, and parked behind it, blocking it in.

The DI was thankful she had had the foresight to wear her Hi-tec Magnum boots, jeans, a shirt, and jumper under her raincoat. She was going to need every one of those layers as the weather worsened. She wasn't looking forward to the climb, but was focussed on the need to save Adrian Jones' life.

More officers were on the way to their location, but the plan for the moment was for the tactical arms team to continue on foot round to the right of the cafe and on up to the top of the falls, positioning themselves to shoot the abductors if negotiations failed.

Yvonne and Dewi were to approach the foot of the falls, and use the megaphone to talk to Carter and Mason.

Her heart thudded in her chest as she fought a rising panic. Now was not the time for an anxiety attack, but the task ahead weighed heavily on them. They couldn't allow anything to go wrong.

"Are you all right, ma'am?" Dewi placed a hand on her shoulder.

She took a deep breath, letting it out slowly through her mouth. "I will be... Come on, flash your warrant card at the guy on the turnstile. I'll explain to the cafe owners what's going on and ask them to keep visitors away. Uniform should arrive soon to block the area off, but we don't need interlopers in the meantime."

"Right you are, ma'am." Dewi passed her the megaphone before waving his badge at the Tan-y-Pistyll cafe attendant in charge of entry to the falls.

He came to meet them.

"DS Dewi Hughes," her sergeant announced. "We're here because we believe a man has been taken to the top of the falls against his will. We are afraid for his safety and intend taking over this area until we resolve the situation. There will be a considerable police presence, I'm afraid, including armed officers. This is DI Yvonne Giles, the officer in charge."

The attendant waved them through. "How long should I close for?" he asked, looking at his watch.

"Until we tell you it's okay to open again, I'm afraid." Dewi tilted his head. "I'm sorry, I know this is affecting your business. We will do what we can to resolve this quickly and safely."

"Do whatever you need to." He pointed to the cafe. "I'll stay inside until you tell me it's over... Good luck."

"Can you see anyone?" Yvonne peered up at the falls towering above them. Two hundred and forty metres of tumbling water. It had an 'O'-shaped funnel, about half-way down, through which the cascading water poured. A spectacular sight. Regarded as one of the seven wonders of Wales, it wasn't unknown for the falls to have upwards of two-thousand visitors a day at the peak of the season. The DI was glad it was much earlier in the year.

Dewi shaded his eyes as he scoured the landscape. "I can't see anyone."

∽

"Me neither." She cranked the handle on the megaphone. It seemed to work though, until she saw Carter and Mason, she couldn't use it. It wouldn't do to scare them off into the woods.

By now, armed officers would near the top and taking their positions.

Below her, she could hear van doors opening and closing, heralding the regular officers. Ambulances would follow them and, in the distance, she could hear the rotary blades of the police helicopter. She hoped it would stay back for the time being.

She cast her eyes around for Dewi, who had vanished.

When he reappeared, it was with two steaming mugs of tea from the cafe. "Thought you might like one of these... It means little cafe under the waterfall," he told her.

"What does?"

"Tan-y-Pistyll."

"Oh, I see. Thanks for the tea." As the warmth from the mug permeated her hand, she realised how cold she had become.

She smiled at her sergeant. "You're a star."

"I try." He grinned. "Get that down you, I'll radio the top, see what they can-"

"We can see them, over," armed response called over the radio. "They're at the head of the waterfall. They should come into your view at any moment. What would you like us to do, over?"

She saw them, standing over the top of the fall. It looked like Carter and Mason were on either side, holding onto Adrian Jones.

The DI swallowed hard. "Dewi, ask them to hold their fire, and stay where they are. I want a chance to talk to the abductors."

"Right you are, ma'am."

She lifted her megaphone. "Peter Carter, can you hear me?" She winced at feedback and moved it further away from her mouth. "My name is DI Yvonne Giles. If you can hear me, please raise your hand."

She couldn't see their expressions and was desperate to gauge their reaction. It would obviously surprise them, having the sudden and massive emergency response. She didn't want that to put AJ at greater risk.

Carter raised his hand.

"Thank you," she sighed with relief. "We're going to place a bag with a radio in, where you can retrieve it, so I can talk to you. If that is okay with you, can you raise your hand?"

For a tense few seconds, Carter didn't move.

A cold sweat developed on her back.

"Dewi?" she asked, "Can you find me a pair of binoculars?"

"Sure." He nodded. "The tactical team are staying put,

until you tell them differently, or they feel an imminent danger to the victim," he confirmed.

"Good. Thank you."

Carter raised his hand.

She raised her megaphone. "Thank you, Peter."

Dewi came back with the binoculars.

"Can you ask the tactical guys to leave the radio about fifteen feet from Carter and Mason, and stand well back? We don't want to agitate them by getting to close."

"Will do. You'll need to set your radio to the alternative frequency, ma'am. I'll sort it and confirm with the tactical team to do the same with the one they hand over."

He adjusted her radio. It wouldn't do to have the kidnappers listen in on their frequency.

"There you go, you're all set." Dewi handed it back to her.

Yvonne adjusted the binoculars until she could clearly see the faces of all three men. AJ looked petrified. His mouth taped up, he looked like a defeated man. The DI thought she saw a wet patch in the front of his trousers.

Her radio scratched and crackled, and Pete Carter's gruff voice came through. "Keep your people back. Don't come any closer. If anything kicks off, he goes over the edge. We came here to do a job. You should walk away and let us have justice."

The DI winced. "I can't walk away, Peter. This wouldn't be justice. This isn't how we sort this out. You should also know that the man you are holding, Adrian Jones, had nothing to do with the death of your daughters. He was not responsible. You would kill an innocent man."

Carter scowled. "You'll say anything to talk us down. I don't care anymore. I want justice for Helen, and Berwyn wants justice for Vicky. We've waited twenty years for you lot to find out what happened. We got sick of waiting."

The noise of water in the background meant concentrating hard on what Carter was saying. Her head throbbed. "You'd be punishing the wrong man. We have your daughter's killer in custody. He will go to trial. You will have your day in court. Believe in that. Please don't hurt anyone else."

Carter pushed AJ closer to the edge.

"Wait, we know we have the right man in the cells. We found Vicky's red backpack."

Mason grabbed the radio from Carter. "You found her bag?"

The DI swallowed. "Yes, Berwyn, we did, and we know we have her killer in custody."

"Did it have Vicky's things in it?"

She could hear the emotion in his voice. "It had some of your daughter's possessions, yes."

"How did she die?"

Yvonne pursed her lips. She ought to steer the conversation away from the girls' deaths. The emotions were too raw and too powerful, the men could lose control. She couldn't tell them that Helen had sustained a broken hyoid bone indicating strangulation, and that they could not confirm how Vicky died.

She cleared her throat. "We can't be sure, yet." She bit her lip, waiting for their response.

Carter took the radio back. "Enough talking, they murdered our daughters. We want justice."

"And you will get it, Peter, trust us. You will have your day in court, and soon. We have charged their killer, and the court will set a date for trial. We'd like you to release Adrian Jones, who is innocent. He was in that photograph only because he was in the wrong place, at the wrong time. Please, let him go? He has family, too."

The police helicopter flew over.

Carter ducked, pulling AJ with him. The terrified man's eyes bulged in their sockets.

"Dewi, contact control and ask them to get that chopper out of here," she shouted, struggling to be heard above the noise of its blades.

"Yes, ma'am," he shouted back, disappearing towards the relative quiet of the cafe interior.

He reappeared a few minutes later, as the helicopter turned around and left. "Sorted."

"Thank you, Dewi."

The DI turned her attention back to the men atop the waterfall. "Please, can you move Mister Jones further from the edge?"

There was no response.

"Are you hungry?" she asked. "We can get you food and hot drinks."

The fact they had a cafe right there meant this was something she could readily achieve. Yvonne crossed her fingers behind her back, muttering, "Come on, come on…"

Carter took several minutes to get back to her. "We'll have sandwiches and a coffee," he barked down the radio. "And don't mess us about. We have nothing more to lose."

"I'm aware of that, Peter. I promise, I will not mess you about. We would like this resolved peacefully, and without further bloodshed."

Dewi's radio crackled. "We've got an unobstructed view of the suspects," the tactical commander advised. "Would you like us to take the shots?"

"Ma'am," he tapped her in the shoulder. "Armed

response could take them both out without harming AJ. They have a clear line of sight."

"No, no..." She held up a hand. "I'm not giving up. I want to bring them all down alive. But, if it looks like they are going to throw him down, then the armed response team must do what they're trained for. Please ask them to give us every chance to end this peacefully."

∽

It took half an hour to get food and drink to three men at the top of the falls. They tasked two regular officers with the job, and Carter gave them further specific instruction, which they followed.

Yvonne blew on her hands to warm fingers stiffened by the cold and the cranking of her radio in the damp air. She shook her limbs to keep the blood flowing, feeling sorry for AJ, who was not dressed for the conditions.

She was still pondering how long the stand-off could continue, when a paramedic approached as though he had read her mind.

He handed her several foil blankets. "We thought they might need these," he said.

"Thank you, I've been worrying about the victim's temperature." She smiled. "We'll get these up there as soon as we can."

"Let us know if you need more." He left.

"I will, thank you," she called after him.

The officers who had taken up the food eventually returned. Both were tight-lipped at the prospect of going back up with blankets, but they accepted the task, turning on their heels and going back the way they had come.

She didn't blame them, conditions were awful, as the drizzle showed no sign of letting up.

The DI jumped as someone tapped her on the shoulder from behind. She almost dropped her radio.

"Sorry, love." It was Tasha.

Yvonne put a hand to her chest to steady her heart. "Hi." She checked her watch. "You scared me. You made great time."

The psychologist grimaced. "I didn't want you dealing with this on your own. I'd like to help, if I'm allowed."

Yvonne nodded. "I'll let the DCI know, I can't see it being a problem, Tasha, not with your experience. It's tense up there. I've been getting nowhere."

"The victim is still alive and kicking. I'd say you're doing an outstanding job."

"We've sent up food and survival blankets. I've been waiting for them to get fed up. I'm not hopeful of making progress until they do."

The psychologist pursed her lips. "You must be shattered yourself, standing out here in this drizzle and murk. Why don't you sit down for a bit?"

Yvonne pulled a face. "I'm only worried about them." She pointed up at the waterfall. "They are all victims. Carter and Mason lost their daughters. They are hurt and angry, and they've become the very thing they despised — cold-blooded killers. Nothing excuses what they've done, but I know they have been through hell, losing their daughters. And, even now, I bet they are secretly regretting the road they have taken. I think they don't know how to pull back. I'm worried they'll think there is no way back. We can't afford to get this wrong. We could end up with all three of them going over the edge. What a mess, Tasha, what a mess."

"And their daughters were Helen and Victoria, correct?"

"That's right, yes."

"I think you are spot on, Yvonne. We need to offer them a way to back down from the position they find themselves in. If you okay it with your DCI, I will talk to them for a while, and see if I can progress things. It will give you a break for a bit."

"Tasha." Dewi gave her a nod on his return. "How are you? Long time, no see."

"I'm good, thank you. How's you? And where's mine?" she grinned, referring to the two mugs of tea he was carrying.

Dewi laughed. "Have this. I'll go beg another." He handed over the mugs. "They'll wonder what I'm playing at," he said, referring to the owners of the cafe. "They've given me these free. I feel cheeky going back for another."

"Please give him our thanks." Yvonne turned her attention back to the falls.

"I bought you a scarf and a hat." Tasha pulled them out of her coat pocket.

"Oh, you are amazing." Yvonne tilted her head. "Thank you for being you."

The psychologist felt the DI's hands. "Put the gloves on now. You need them."

An urgent message came over Dewi's radio. "They're making their way back to the edge, over."

"No." Yvonne cranked her radio. "Peter, can you hear me? Peter?"

A voice came through on Dewi's radio. "Do we take the shot, over?"

The DI flicked a sideways glance at her sergeant. "Tell them no, not yet."

Tasha approached Yvonne, holding out her hand. "May I?"

The DI searched her partner's face. "Are you sure?"

She nodded. "Yes."

Yvonne handed the radio over.

∽

"Mister Carter? Peter? My name is Doctor Natasha Phillips. How are you doing up there?"

"We don't need a doctor," Carter snapped. "It's time we finished what we started."

As Yvonne watched via the binoculars, Carter moved AJ in front of him. She gasped.

"Peter..." Tasha remained calm. "You and your friend..." She looked that the DI.

"Berwyn," the DI confirmed.

"Yourself and your friend, Berwyn, have been to hell and back over the loss of your girls."

"They were murdered," he growled.

"Yes, they were, and this has been the toughest time of your lives. You have experienced what no parent ever should. We none of us here can truly know what you have suffered, but we empathise, and we care. I would not try to minimise what you have been through, but committing one more murder will not make it right. It cannot change what happened. Taking the life of this man will not bring back your girls, but you can honour Helen and Vicky's memory by doing the right thing, and letting this man go. That is what they would want you to do. Their killer is in custody, and will spend the rest of his life in prison. He will feel the full weight of the law. Your girls will have justice, and you will have your day in court to hear it. Helen and Vicky would want you to let go of this now, and set this innocent man free."

Mason said something to Carter. Yvonne wished she could lip read. She informed Tasha.

The psychologist waited a moment before continuing. "Peter... Berwyn, we'd like you to move away from the edge of the falls, and take..." She looked at the DI.

"Adrian."

"Take Adrian back too. We have more blankets, food, and hot drinks waiting down here for you. You can all come down safely."

The men continued to confer, arguing amongst themselves.

Carter did not look happy, but Mason looked as though he had had enough. He began moving AJ back from the edge.

The DI held her breath.

Carter moved to grab AJ away from Berwyn.

A shot rang out.

Carter stumbled back, clutching the arm with which he had tried to grab AJ.

"We're giving up!" Berwyn's voice shook. "Don't shoot! We're coming down."

24

FALLOUT

"Are you all right, Yvonne?" DCI Llewelyn joined her in the main office after she finished writing up statements.

She stood at the window, looking out over the park in Newtown, and the trees swaying in the wind, lost in thought.

"Yvonne?"

She turned, her mind slowly returning to the present. "Sorry?"

"How are you? I bet you're exhausted."

The DI sighed, her eyes glazed.

"I wanted to congratulate you on a job well done." He tilted his head. "You saved the hostage's life, and three murderers are now in custody. Well done for catching Wyatt, that's another cold case closed, thanks to your hard work."

"It was a mess, sir." She closed her eyes. "Four lives lost, and for what? For Wyatt, it was the need to posses people he couldn't otherwise. For Carter and Mason, it was the need for revenge."

She perched on the edge of the nearest desk. "You know, because of anxiety, I have a tendency to over-analyse things... My feelings, the things I want, the things I think I know. I always thought it was a millstone around my neck but, when I see the damage impulsive behaviour can wreak, I'm glad I take my time, even if I drive myself crazy."

The DCI nodded. "So am I. I always know you'll do the right thing. And it isn't for us to analyse why some people act as they do. I leave that to the psychologists. It's our job to protect the vulnerable and make sure we put away the bad guys. And you and your team achieved that today."

"They're saying we missed something."

"Who are?" Llewelyn frowned.

"The press. Perhaps, they're right."

"In what way?"

"We interviewed Wyatt on at least two occasions before Carter and Mason killed Simon Wells. If only we had searched his property sooner..."

Llewelyn placed a hand on her arm. "You know, and I know, that the court would not have granted a warrant sooner. We didn't have enough evidence. Neither could you have done more than you did. You, your team, and Tasha. And, but the way, they are all waiting for you in my office."

"What?" She raised her brows.

"We're having a shandy to celebrate."

"A shandy?" She laughed, a solid chuckle that came from her belly. "Boy, you know how to push the boat out."

He grinned. "Well, you know, most of us have to drive home later."

"So, you're basically offering this amazing team lemonade with a sniff of lager."

"Yeah, basically..."

She laughed again, "I can't think of anything else I'd rather have."

A cheer went up from Dewi, Callum, Dai, and Tasha as she entered with the DCI.

Dewi poured the drinks, and they toasted the successful conclusion of the case.

Yvonne lifted her glass. "To you lot, I couldn't wish to work with a better bunch."

∼

"PENNY FOR THEM?" Tasha asked as they walked along the promenade at Aberystwyth.

The early April sun beat down from a pure blue sky. It was promising to be the warmest day of the year so far.

The sea calmly massaged the shore, and the many socially distanced, mask-wearing visitors basked in their newfound freedom from lockdown.

"You know," Yvonne took Tasha's hand. "This is one of my favourite places to be."

The psychologist smiled, squeezing her partner's hand. "Mine, too. We've created memories here…"

"Thank you." The DI turned to her.

"For what?"

"Ending the siege at the falls. You were amazing."

Tasha pulled a face. "You did all the hard work. I got in on the glory."

"Yeah, right?"

"Seriously, your patience won out, Yvonne. Yours, and all those out there with you. I only helped so you could rest. Berwyn Mason was already at the point of giving up. You did that, DI Yvonne Giles, and I love you."

Yvonne linked her arm through Tasha's. "Shall we get some food?"

"Let's… It's your turn to buy."

"Is it?"

The psychologist laughed. "No, but I thought it was worth a try."

The DI laughed with her, feeling more relaxed than she had in weeks. "Thank heavens for you, the sun, and for love," was her reply.

∼

THE END

AFTERWORD

Mailing list: You can join my emailing list here : AnnamarieMorgan.com

Facebook page: AnnamarieMorganAuthor

You might also like to read the other books in the series:
Book 1: Death Master:

After months of mental and physical therapy, Yvonne Giles, an Oxford DI, is back at work and that's just how she likes it. So when she's asked to hunt the serial killer responsible for taking apart young women, the DI jumps at the chance but hides the fact she is suffering debilitating flashbacks. She is told to work with Tasha Phillips, an in-her-face, criminal psychologist. The DI is not enamoured with the idea. Tasha has a lot to prove. Yvonne has a lot to get over. A tentative link with a 20 year-old cold case brings them closer to the truth but events then take a horrifyingly personal turn.

Book 2: You Will Die

After apprehending an Oxford Serial Killer, and almost losing her life in the process, DI Yvonne Giles has left England for a quieter life in rural Wales.Her peace is shattered when she is asked to hunt a priest-killing psychopath, who taunts the police with messages inscribed on the corpses.Yvonne requests the help of Dr. Tasha Phillips, a psychologist and friend, to aid in the hunt. But the killer is one step ahead and the ultimatum, he sets them, could leave everyone devastated.

Book 3: Total Wipeout

A whole family is wiped out with a shotgun. At first glance, it's an open-and-shut case. The dad did it, then killed himself. The deaths follow at least two similar family wipeouts – attributed to the financial crash.

So why doesn't that sit right with Detective Inspector Yvonne Giles? And why has a rape occurred in the area, in the weeks preceding each family's demise? Her seniors do not believe there are questions to answer. DI Giles must therefore risk everything, in a high-stakes investigation ofa mysterious masonic ring and players in high finance.

Can she find the answers, before the next innocent family is wiped out?

Book 4: Deep Cut

In a tiny hamlet in North Wales, a female recruit is murdered whilst on Christmas home leave. Detective Inspector Yvonne Giles is asked to cut short her own leave, to investigate. Why was the young soldier killed? And is her death related to several alleged suicides at her army base? DI Giles this it is, and that someone powerful has a dark secret they will do anything to hide.

Book 5: The Pusher

Young men are turning up dead on the banks of the River Severn. Some of them have been missing for days or even weeks. The only thing the police can be sure of, is that the men have drowned. Rumours abound that a mythical serial killer has turned his attention from the Manchester canal to the waterways of Mid-Wales. And now one of CID's own is missing. A brand new recruit with everything to live for. DI Giles must find him before it's too late.

Book 6: Gone

Children are going missing. They are not heard from again until sinister requests for cryptocurrency go viral. The public must pay or the children die. For lead detective Yvonne Giles, the case is complicated enough. And then the unthinkable happens...

Book 7: Bone Dancer

A serial killer is murdering women, threading their bones back together, and leaving them for police to find. Detective Inspector Yvonne Giles must find him before more innocent victims die. Problem is, the killer wants her and will do anything he can to get her. Unaware that she, herself, is is a target, DI Giles risks everything to catch him.

Book 8: Blood Lost

A young man comes home to find his whole family missing. Half-eaten breakfasts and blood spatter on the lounge wall are the only clues to what happened...

Book 9: Angel of Death

He is watching. Biding his time. Preparing himself for a

torturous kill. Soaring above; lord of all. His journey, direct through the lives of the unsuspecting.

The Angel of Death is nigh.

The peace of the Mid-Wales countryside is shattered, when a female eco-warrior is found crucified in a public wood. At first, it would appear a simple case of finding which of the woman's enemies had had her killed. But DI Yvonne Giles has no idea how bad things are going to get. As the body count rises, she will need all of her instincts, and the skills of those closest to her, to stop the murderous rampage of the Angel of Death.

Book 10: Death in the Air

Several fatal air collisions have occurred within a few months in rural Wales. According to the local Air Accidents Investigation Branch (AAIB) inspector, it's a coincidence. Clusters happen. Except, this cluster is different. DI Yvonne Giles suspects it when she hears some of the witness statements but, when an AAIB inspector is found dead under a bridge, she knows it.

Something is way off. Yvonne is determined to get to the bottom of the mystery, but exactly how far down the treacherous rabbit hole is she prepared to go?

Book 11: Death in the Mist

The morning after a viscous sea-mist covers the seaside town of Aberystwyth, a young student lies brutalised within one hundred yards of the castle ruins.

DI Yvonne Giles' reputation precedes her. Having successfully captured more serial killers than some detectives have caught colds, she is seconded to head the murder investigation team, and hunt down the young woman's killer.

What she doesn't know, is this is only the beginning...

Book 12: Death under Hypnosis

When the secretive and mysterious Sheila Winters approaches Yvonne Giles and tells her that she murdered someone thirty years before, she has the DI's immediate attention.

Things get even more strange when Sheila states:

She doesn't know who.

She doesn't know where.

She doesn't know why.

Book 13: Fatal Turn

A seasoned hiker goes missing from the Dolfor Moors after recording a social media video describing a narrow cave he intends to explore. A tragic accident? Nothing to see here, until a team of cavers disappear on a coastal potholing expedition, setting off a string of events that has DI Giles tearing her hair out. What, or who is the thread that ties this series of disappearances together?

A serial killer, thriller murder-mystery set in Wales.

Book 14: The Edinburgh Murders

A newly-retired detective from the Met is murdered in a murky alley in Edinburgh, a sinister calling card left with the body.

The dead man had been a close friend of psychologist Tasha Phillips, giving her her first gig with the Met decades before.

Tasha begs DI Yvonne Giles to aid the Scottish police in solving the case.

In unfamiliar territory, and with a ruthless killer haunting the streets, the DI plunges herself into one of the darkest, most terrifying cases of her career. Who exactly is The Poet?

Remember to watch out for Book 16, coming soon...

Printed in Great Britain
by Amazon